SOCIAL
DISEASE

SOCIAL DISEASE

Paul Rudnick

ALFRED A. KNOPF
NEW YORK 1986

THIS IS A BORZOI BOOK
PUBLISHED BY ALFRED A. KNOPF, INC.

Library of Congress Cataloging-in-Publication Data

Rudnick, Paul.
  Social disease.
  I. Title.
PS3568.U334S63 1986   813'.54   85-45775
ISBN 0-394-55270-9

Manufactured in the United States of America
FIRST EDITION

For my mother, my father and my brother

SOCIAL
DISEASE

1

The Fabulous Club de

"Brucie, we gotta get in. I told Joyce we was gonna get in."

"Hey, Debbie, put a sock in it, willya? We're gettin' in, don't worry, Bruce Kokokowski don't take shit from nobody."

"Oh, *right,*" said Michelle. "Oh, *sure.* Tell me *another.*"

There were hundreds of people in the street, waiting outside the fabulous Club de. Bruce, Debbie and Michelle had been standing for almost an hour, ever since arriving in Manhattan from Piscataway, New Jersey. The crowd surged forward. People were jammed in twenty deep, shoulder to shoulder, straining to see, as if there were a fistfight going on.

Debbie and Michelle were sisters. Debbie, a high-school senior, wore a new dress, in bouncy lime green polyester. Debbie was pretty, and shrill.

Twelve-year-old Michelle had slept on the bus all the way into the city. She still wore her knit ski pajamas, the ones with the reindeer print, and moccasins.

Bruce, Debbie's boyfriend, had one of those pulpy New Jersey faces, like a slab of raw meat. The Manuel Elegante trademark was sewn onto all of Bruce's clothing. The trademark was a map of New Jersey with a handlebar moustache.

"This is being the Club of de?" asked Salima, eagerly.

"Of course it is being," said haughty Ramira. "We are being for the boogie."

"I am being with the get down," said Latinda, adjusting the folds of her chador.

"It is too much the excitement!" said Salima. "I am having the spinning in the head!"

"Wives of Fadood," came the crackle from the limousine's intercom. "With the quiet you are being!"

The limousine inched its way toward the Club's entrance, bludgeoning taxis and members of the crowd. Debbie pressed her face to the car's tinted windows. The limousine came to a stop, and a team of bodyguards leapt out. Debbie sighed and wished she could have bodyguards; she soulfully coveted a life worth threatening. The bodyguards formed a cordon, batting Debbie to one side. Sheik Oded Ben Fadood, the Arab oil potentate, and his six wives were ushered through the crowd and into the Club.

Fadood strode ahead of the wives, his goatee oozing with the oil of his last twenty orgies, his bulk heaving beneath a rank burnoose, encrusted with unraveling gold embroidery and grimy copper amulets. The wives were smothered in ritual dress, in billowy black gauze sacks which hid their tempting, unclean flesh. Only their eyes remained vaguely visible, peeking out from behind black wrap-around sunglasses.

This was Fadood's first night at the Club de. The wives had twittered of nothing else, as the Club had been roundly condemned down at the mosque.

"It is being too much the beautiful!" cried Salima, entering the Club.

"I am shaking my booty!" declared Cardima, repeating a phrase from an American song she had heard on the radio.

"Praise be to Allah!" belched Oded Ben Fadood. "Is funky town!"

Guy Huber tumbled from a taxi and stood at the edge of the crowd, which had begun to vibrate with trauma. Guy yawned and tried to shake the sleep from his brain. Although it was almost midnight, Guy had just awakened. Guy was a boy about town, so he hoarded his more alert hours for the night, when something was up.

Guy knew that if he stood off to one side and looked unconcerned, he would be noticed immediately. Sure enough, the man on the door nodded at Guy and held up a hand. Guy squeezed through the crowd, his entrance assured.

Guy had nice teeth, a plus in any mammal. He had only recently abandoned wearing an onyx tuxedo stud in his left ear, now that everyone and their lawyer were doing it. There was still a hole in Guy's ear, and he occasionally hung a tea bag from it. Tonight Guy was dressed as an urban savage, a rowdy, a road warrior. He had on tight black jeans, sublimely faded and molded to torniquet. His T-shirt had been washed and bleached until it just drooped and draped, like a rag; the T-shirt was printed with the Japanese characters for life, death and shoes. Over these exquisite tatters, Guy wore a black leather biker's jacket, bristling with studs and zippers; Guy had hacked off a sleeve at the shoulder, to look as if he'd been in a vicious accident. Guy always wore black, in order to appear dangerous.

Guy had the look of a child as the curtain rises, at the theater. He had a long face, and his mouth would hang a bit open in wonder, until he remembered to close it. Guy's eyebrows were set high on his forehead, in perpetual surprise, and his eyes shone.

Guy was always happy. He saw no reason not to be. Guy knew

that people might think he was a dolt, or mentally deficient, but there it was. Guy was Pollyanna in leather.

Guy had been married a few days back, to Venice, the most marvelous girl. Guy was crazy for Venice, shakingly in love. He had been trying desperately to express his passion, to announce it, to show Venice just how he felt. That afternoon, inspiration had struck, and Guy had added a wide blue streak to his black hair.

The streak was a neon tint, like the highlight on a comic-book superhero's hair. Guy had decided the color was an eternal blue, a Venice blue. The streak was styled to spike up, like a Cherokee's feather or a tiny bolt of lightning. Guy couldn't wait for Venice to see the streak; he hadn't caught her all day, but he knew she'd end up at the Club. The couple had met at the Club, they'd practically been married there. They could never find each other at home; they'd leave messages and notes and clues. Manhattan is a board game, Chutes and Ladders, and making contact takes time and energy. But husbands can always find wives, Guy thought; that's what marriage is all about! I love my streak, Guy sang to himself, and I love my wife! I love 'em!

"Why's he gettin' in?" Bruce asked. "He looks like shit."

"Brucie, be quiet," said Debbie, "he'll hear you."

"What, the guy wit' the blue hair? He's inside awready."

"*No*, the doorman," said Debbie, gazing at the young man who stood by the red velvet rope.

"Fuck, that asshole? I want him to hear me! Hey, ASSHOLE!"

"Nice play, Shakespeare," giggled Michelle.

"He's not an asshole," said Debbie, furious. "He's ultra-max! I read about him in the paper. He's worked here for two weeks, he likes redheads and movies and . . . Brucie, I can't remember! I can't remember his favorite recording artist!"

"Hey, BEANHEAD, ya got some PEOPLE HERE!"

. . .

The Club de was the club of the moment, the latest temple of exclusive yet violently publicized depravity. It was impossible to pick up a newspaper, let alone a telephone, without catching word of the Club's reign of glamour.

The Club de had once been the Loew's Artesian, a Depression-era movie palace. The theater had been a grand Babylonian affair, a ravishing pile of Ali Baba kitsch. Moviegoers had jammed the plush velvet seats, sighing over Garbo's latest, swooning with Swanson, all to the chug of The Mighty Wurlitzer.

Then television had come along. The Artesian had been converted for live broadcasts of ragingly popular game shows. As Studio A-16, the theater had been seen nationwide in black and white, as Quiz Kids sweated over cash jackpots, mink and Trips for Two to Beautiful Diamond Head.

Scandal ensued, and the theater had been shuttered, under allegations of graft and payola and other national pastimes. The shell sat vacant for years, the marquee was destroyed, before it could rot and fall on someone. The interior flaked and peeled. Some people wanted to tear the place down; others suggested landmark status. Six months ago a group of suspect businessmen had bought the property, and restoration had begun.

Guy Huber headed through the lobby of the Club de, which was mirrored and marbled and kept in hushed gloom. Palm leaves swayed overhead and people whispered. The lobby was all anticipation, and Guy felt a shiver. He was drawn to the mirror, for a tug at his streak. He turned his head this way and that, scowling and hollowing his cheeks, imitating a fashion model.

He left his leather jacket with a pair of chattering usherettes, who manned the coatcheck, located in what was once the Artesian's concession stand.

"Hi, Guy," said the coatcheck girls. "We love your jacket."

"Thanks," said Guy. "Isn't it neat? Don't I look like I'm going to beat people up? Should I get, like, a big scar?"

"Ooooh, yes," said the coatcheck girls. "We love your hair."

"Do you really like it?" asked Guy, concerned. "Have you seen Venice?"

"Somewhere," said the coatcheck girls helpfully.

Guy scampered on, and the Club de erupted before him.

The theater's screen remained, serving as the blank canvas against which the evening would occur. The orchestra seating had been removed and a dance floor installed, so abused that it had to be resurfaced every two weeks. Due to the early hour, only a few haphazard couples were dancing.

The sloping mezzanine had also been gutted and then lined with a dull gray industrial material. A central bar had been cre-ated from the Artesian's pipe organ. The bartenders were mus-clemen, shirtless and oiled. They behaved like frat-house jocks, greeting Guy with thumbs-up signals and shouts of "Hey, dude!"

"Hi, guys," said Guy. "How are you?"

"Awesome, dude," said the bartenders, tossing Guy a beer.

"Have you guys seen Venice?" asked Guy, picking his beer up off the floor.

"Around," said the bartenders, who also loved Venice. "Way to go, dude."

Guy looked up. The domed cathedral ceiling was etched with a midnight blue map of the heavens, the constellations forming outlines of stars of the thirties. Much of this was obscured by a grid of pipe and cable, which held the Club's lighting instru-ments. These instruments were novelty pieces, installed many stories above the dance floor. There were the fiendish, darting lasers, sharp blades of ectoplasmic green light; there were the orgasmic red police alerts, whirring as if at the scene of a homi-cide; there were the poles of yellow construction lamps, which could be lowered to rotate ominously between the dancers' bodies; and there were the flickering strobes, said to cause epileptic seizures, and no help at all in finding wives or misplaced contact lenses.

Guy leaned against a stalwart Corinthian column, sipping his beer. The column was topped with a disc jockey's booth, a mire of albums and dials and headphones set in a winged chariot. The disc jockeys monitored the health of the dance floor, selecting, mixing and amplifying the evening's music. Guy respected the disc jockeys; he considered them Olympians, hurtling bolts of throb and blast at the mortals below.

The Club's most powerful element was darkness. There were no windows, and the overall lighting was kept caressingly inky. A human face had no choice but to glow, like a pearl in an elegant jeweler's case. Lately Guy had begun to suspect that daylight did not even exist.

"It is being too much the wonderfulness," said Latinda, her body a churning pillar of cloth as she shimmied beside the dance floor.

"The men who are being without the shirts," said Cardima, "they are giving me the beer, dude!"

"I am being the party animal!" cried Hofstra, hopping frantically to the beat, the bounce of her sunglasses revealing flashes of glistening, kohl-rimmed eye.

"Wives!" cautioned Hassad, a tall, glowering Arab. Hassad was Oded Ben Fadood's lieutenant, and his fine French tailoring concealed a potent bullwhip.

"Fun! Fun!" bellowed Oded Ben Fadood, lifting his burnoose high over his sagging thighs, as he performed a resounding stomp dance with his current favorite, a small, disinterested goat.

Fadood, given his simple peasant nature, might have been the picture of robust good cheer, of innocent, ignorant thirst. Defying the examples of Zorba, Tevye and so many persuasively earthy fictions, he was not. Fadood was a barbaric poor man, enabled by circumstance to become a barbaric rich man. The discovery of oil on his humble patch of desert had only increased his circle of abuse. Where once Fadood had thieved the sandals of his neighbor, he now purchased full city blocks. As Fadood had abandoned defiled local girls, he now discarded sports cars which had run out of gas. None of this disturbed Fadood, who was as happy as any bulldozer.

"Oogie-oogie-boogie!" thundered Fadood, leeringly spraying Contessa Larini with the contents of his battered pig bladder (the sack held a Montrachet '64, so the Contessa was not all that offended).

Guy surveyed the murk. He knew Venice was here somewhere. Venice was a favorite at the Club; her mail was often delivered right to the bar. Guy heard someone call "Darling!" in a wickedly insinuating tone. As he turned, he felt a hand prowl under his T-shirt, from behind.

"Venice!" Guy cried, but wait—this couldn't be Venice's hand; the fingernails were too long, the touch too lewd. Why, it was Licky Banes, lusting for cash and saying hello.

"Hi, Licky!" said Guy, squirming free.

"Guy!" said Licky, "I've been looking everywhere for you. I've got to ask you something. I have to know, I *must* know— have you ever peed on anyone? I mean, as a favor?"

"Gee, I don't think so," said Guy. He was never sure just how to answer Licky's questions.

"Oh," said Licky, disappointed. "Don't you do *anything?*"

Licky was blondish and sliver thin. He seemed entirely streamlined, a Deco objet, all exaggerated profile. He had a bold, sharp nose, a beak with the hauteur of the Chrysler Building. His eyes sat high on either side, like earrings. His hair fell in thatchy waves, and he had elongated, marionette hands. "I'm a coathanger," he would announce, bending with the breeze.

Licky refused categorization. When asked to choose between *M* and *F* on a census form, he had scribbled *V*. When children taunted him in the street, he would claim he was their real father. Licky's ambition was to become a still photograph, a glossy 8 x 10 processed by a master retoucher. To this end he sought the ideal pose. Tonight he wore an effortless cream flannel suit, of an Oxford bag; he had placed three bright yellow Ticonderoga pencils in the breast pocket, just because. Licky was attitude incarnate, picture an extremely well-dressed exclamation point.

"Guy," said Licky, deliberately ignoring Guy's streak, as a sign of approval, "if you had to eat a baby, where would you start? I mean, really?"

"Boy," said Guy, "I don't know. It's hard to say. Licky, have you seen Venice?"

"Venice? Has she left you? Already? So very soon? Wait, tell me everything. Was it sordid, was it deeply offensive? Did you call each other bitterly personal things which can never be forgiven, and throw toaster ovens? Is it soul-wrenching, do you feel useless, and impotent, and discarded? Wait, there's someone—is that her?"

Guy squinted across the hall. He could make out a woman's figure, but the woman seemed too tall to be Venice. Licky craned his neck and stared. Licky loved to stare at people; he lacked only a diamond cutter's loupe. The woman touched her breast and gave a fetching little wave, the sort of gesture often followed by the phrase "Yoo-hoo!"

"Lucy!" Licky called. "Devil thing!"

Lucy Yates Membrane was a Harvard boy in the throes of a transsexual procedure. Tonight Lucy wore a tartan-print hostess skirt with ornamental safety pin, a frilly lace blouse with jabot and cameo, and black patent pumps with a thin gold band at the heel. Her hair was drawn up in a holiday chignon, with an impetuous sprig of holly added as she left the house. There was a softness to Lucy, a nostalgic passivity. Given today's independent young women, Lucy's models were an open question. Lucy looked and behaved most like your genteel maiden aunt, surrounded by her antimacassars and whatnots, if only your maiden aunt had been well over six feet tall and large-boned.

"Hello, boys," she said, offering the firm silicone of her cheekbone. "It's been too long."

While Licky all but devoured Lucy's flesh, Guy decided to shake her hand. Guy was Yale, after all.

"Hi, Lucy!" said Guy. "You look great! I like your holly. Have you seen Venice?"

"Guy, stop dreaming, you must accept the loss as inevitable, perhaps pre-ordained, now, look at Lucy here," said Licky, "here's someone who knows about *loss*. Lucy, Guy's dying to know, after they, you know, hack it off, do you get to keep it? Or do *they* hang on to it—are there just absolute *bins* of penises sitting around somewhere?"

"No, dear, I haven't seen Venice," said Lucy. "I hope everything's all right. Take care."

"My," said Licky, at Lucy's retreat. "Aren't *we* the touchy little grab-bag. I mean, if I had mine cut off, I'd tell everything. I'd have it done just for *conversation*. All right, now you just sit here and I'll find your little woman, Lord knows in what raw port or squalid back alley. Now, swallow this and don't worry about a thing."

Licky put a merry red capsule into Guy's hand, and his tongue into Guy's ear, and ran off, desperate to voice the evening's first opinion on Guy's streak.

"Bye, Licky," said Guy. "Thanks!"

An hour passed, and Guy found no trace of his wife. He was not worried, just in love. Where could she be? Caught in after-theater traffic? The all-night deli? Curaçao? Venice was an active girl, and sometimes she told Guy where she was going while Guy was asleep. The gallery opening! Of course!

Brace Farnum had been exhibiting his celebrity portraits tonight. Venice must've been there, Brace had painted her earlier in the week. The portraits were executed in actual cosmetics, in eyeshadows and eyeliners and loose powder. The opening had been a triumph. Caronia Desti, Fashion's Oracle, and Tanzo Matta, the designer, had caught the first cab uptown to the Club.

"Guy!" Caronia trilled, spotting the streak. "Crunchable!"

Caronia was a legend, and probably a myth, more calligraphy than flesh in her yards of Kabuki silk. Caronia was ancient, perhaps 100, perhaps more, certainly someone who had witnessed the coming of both fire and The Rich Gypsy Look.

"Hi, Caronia," said Guy. "Hi, Tanzo. How was the opening? I wish I'd gone but I was asleep. Was it terrific?"

"Blue!" Caronia continued. "Prussian! Periwinkle! A calliope of color!"

Caronia was the editrix of *Glaze,* which was a leading lifestyle publication and the source of her syntax. *Glaze* considered "life" and "style" to be synonymous. The magazine was printed on the glossiest paper, the huge photos splayed at jolting angles. *Glaze* looked good on the coffee table, or carried. *Glaze* was information to wear.

"But you can wear blue," Caronia told Guy. "You have the skin of a Benedictine!"

"I do? Really?" said Guy, delighted. Before he could ask about Venice, Caronia was off, smooching the air on either side of his head, as if preferring his two imaginary companions.

"Bye, Caronia!" said Guy. "Have fun!"

Caronia's arrival signaled the evening's true build. It was almost 2 a.m., so people could show up without seeming too sincere. The very latest to arrive were the ubiquitous Children Of, in a flurry of apologies and custom-made cowboy boots.

The Children Of are the offspring of famous people. The Children Of were late because they had attended their parents' dinner parties, where they had referred to ambassadors and Nobel laureates as "Jack" and "Aunt Bobo." Everyone liked the Children Of; they were honored as relics, splinters of The True Cross, bone fragments from the little toe of a Gabor.

"Think about it," said Licky, goosing Guy with a swizzle stick. "These are the people they let *in.* "

"Youccch!" said Guy, goosed.

Then, still loosely in search of Venice, Licky scrawled his phone number across a nude busboy and surged on. Guy noticed that the busboy had another message on his shoulder. It read, "Guy—I'm at de," and it was signed with Venice's initial and her lipstick blot. It wouldn't be long now!

"Hey, CROTCH ROT!"

"Brucie, I'm not going to stand here if you keep this up, it's just really gross, you don't know anything about being sociable!"

"Hey, PUSSY!"

"Are those men?" asked Michelle, pointing.

"HEY, HEINIEBITER NUMBER ONE!"

"Latinda, that is not being a woman," said Cardima, as the harem eyed Lucy Yates Membrane.

"It is being a *large* woman," said Tira, as they edged toward the spot where Lucy stood at the bar sipping a diet soft drink.

"You are being the what?" asked Hofstra, studiously fingering Lucy's skirt, two horse blankets worth of plaid.

"I beg your pardon?" said Lucy.

"You are shaking your groove thing?" asked Ramira, who was watching the dance floor.

"What?" said Lucy.

"You are being the foxy lady," rumbled Oded Ben Fadood,

who panted for a sturdy ankle. He gazed at Lucy hungrily, all but pawing the carpet with a hoof. So much woman, he thought to himself, so much! "Boom chicky boom!" he volunteered.

"Oh, Mr. Fadood," Lucy tittered, recognizing the swarthy primitive, said to be worth so many billions. "Stop it!"

Guy wanted to sit down. He had been mingling for what seemed like decades. He knew Venice was on her way. If he stayed in one place, he might be easier for her to spot. The area around the dance floor was lined with banquettes, silvery structures, low and underslung.

Guy plotted his siege. As soon as the man with the boa constrictor stood up, Guy dove for his place. Guy stretched out, almost parallel to the floor, in one of those agreeable positions considered very bad for the spine.

"Forget dot vumman," breathed Ratallia Parv, the angelic Austrian film star, scrunching in beside Guy. Ratallia was artless tonight, in a football jersey, a garter belt and a thousand-dollar Tanzo skirt.

"Hi, Ratallia," said Guy. "How are you? Do you need more room?"

Ratallia was a true star, known for her media coverage far more than for any acting ability. She was still in her teens, but had made thousands of films, in every language. Ratallia had a habit of expressing almost every emotion through nudity.

"I dunt lick jore country," said Ratallia, arching her throat, which she'd been told was effective. "Chu dunt unnerstand vimmen. A vimmen neets loave. Are ju varing a bilt?"

"Ratallia," said Guy, politely, "I barely know you."

"No vun knows Ratallia. Chust millions. Dey vant her. Dey dunt unnerstand. All dey vant is boozums, boozums and wagina."

"Wagina?" said Guy.

"Wagina," said Ratallia, sadly. "But Ratallia, che is more.

Che is like de sea. I write pome jabout it. I write many pome. Ju vant to read Ratallia's pome?"

"Ratallia, I'm married," said Guy. It's handy being married, Guy thought. Guy liked Ratallia's films well enough, but after seeing more than two of them, he felt he *had* slept with her.

Ratallia sighed and rolled away, toward Jon Gelle, who lolled at the far end of the banquette. Gelle was also a film star, an American, known for his squint, his forearms and his desire for privacy, which required his attendance at the Club de at least five nights a week.

Outside, the temperature dropped below freezing. The crowd filled the block, cutting off traffic. Bruce, Debbie and Michelle were hemmed in by other people's bodies. Their arms were pinned to their sides. Michelle's nose was running, so she wiped it on a nearby sleeve.

"Buddy, you're askin' for it," Bruce snarled at the doorman. "I been here three fuckin' hours and you been lettin' them GEEKS in! What is your fuckin' PROBLEM?"

"Excuse me," said Debbie, "I don't even know him, he's just standing next to me, do you guys need coffee or something, I could run down to the corner . . ."

"Brucie, you are really like the dumbest person in the whole world I ever met," said Michelle. "You're never gonna get in, never ever, it's cold, why don't we just go play Ms. Pac-Man, huh? This place is stupid, I bet ya they don't even *got* Ms. Pac-Man!"

"I'M ASKIN' YA ONE MORE TIME, PORKTURD, YA LET US IN OR I TAKE YOUR FUCKIN' FACE OFF!"

"Brucie, take it back, take the corsage, and the ring, and when I get home I'm taking the Pink Panther doll and burning it, and the keychain with the pom-pom, and the poster with the two seagulls, you can just have it! I never want to see you again, and your eyes are too close together, I lied! Look, everybody, his eyes are so close together it's like one big EYE! If you had normal human BEING eyes, we'd get IN!"

Inside, Guy stood at the railing of the Artesian's balcony. He watched the dancers below pounding the floor and tossing their limbs around. They looked like they were being shot.

Guy could not spot Venice among the dancers. He longed to dance with her; his hips began to shift, called by the music. He turned, checking the balcony itself. He saw mostly couples, fighting or dozing or making love.

Returning to the balcony rail, Guy scanned the banquettes, and he caught a glimpse of the tightest leather miniskirt. I know that skirt! Guy thought. He felt like Robinson Crusoe, at the discovery of Friday's footprints. The island is not deserted, Guy exulted; there's life!

"Darling!" Guy heard, through the din, and he ran for the grand mahogany staircase which led downstairs. Guy arrived, breathless, beside an urn at the foot of the stair. Then he saw Venice's leg, wearing someone's wristwatch, headed for the dance floor.

As Guy followed the leg, he felt bits of confetti fall onto his hair. A mechanism in the lighting grid had begun to sift a ton of artificial snow onto the dancers, as if the Club were set in a crystal dome and had been turned upside down and shaken. The dancers were enchanted by the effect, but tried desperately not to show it. Their expressions said, Oh, but you should have been here Halloween, when we bobbed for emeralds, or Tuesday, when we molested the twins.

Licky's voice howled an octave above the rest, "Napalm!"

The Olympic slalom team schussed in, and Caronia Desti led the bartenders in a scintillating rendition of "Frosty The Snowman," in Urdu.

Finally, ten whitened women stripped and formed a pyramid, at which everyone rolled their eyes, as if they'd been asked to avoid stepping on their mothers' corpses, or wear bell-bottoms.

"Darling!" Guy heard, and he looked up through the whirling sparkle. High above his head stretched an iron catwalk, a spidery skein of black metal which spanned the hall. The catwalk allowed workmen to change bulbs and to re-paint, yet it seemed far from practical, more of a tightrope. At the center of the catwalk stood the most desirable girl in Manhattan.

"Venice!" Guy cried.

"Whoa," she called. "It's snowing!" She grabbed a magnum of champagne from one of the nine men who surrounded her. She leaned far out and poured; Guy was able to catch a few drops on his tongue. Venice leaned down to kiss Guy, but the nine men caught her just in time, before she could plunge the twenty feet to where her husband stood.

"Hi!" said Guy. "I know you!"

Venice was wearing her black leather miniskirt, and a loose white cashmere sweater with a deep V neck. As she swung down the metal stair, the sweater dropped off one shoulder. Venice was always spilling out of her clothes. Everything in her wardrobe was either skintight or loose and teasing. Venice always wore sheer black stockings and the most sadistic high heels. She dressed to arouse.

Venice was luscious. She had real curves and real cleavage. She had a stunning face, set off by a broad, lascivious grin. She had an indefinable hairstyle, a swag of thick blonde dazzle that seemed always in motion, falling in her eyes, getting caught in her mouth. Venice spoke in a husky growl, with a deep, filthy laugh.

Venice was no stranger to flirtation; she was practically no stranger to anyone. She smoldered, even at breakfast. Venice—at times literally—enjoyed a love affair with Manhattan.

As Guy watched Venice descend, he went completely to

pieces. His knees wobbled and his face went slack. Venice saw this and started to growl.

Venice paused for a second at the bottom of the stair, just to drive Guy completely wild.

"Venice . . ." Guy babbled, helplessly.

"Yes?" Venice replied. Then she laughed, and ran to Guy and kissed him. Guy whimpered.

When the Hubers kissed, people could tell they were in love; everyone wanted to look away, or buy tickets. A remnant of the Club's years as a television studio remained: an APPLAUSE sign rigged atop the theater's proscenium. As Guy and Venice kissed, the sign flashed and the crowd went mad.

"Hi, hubby," said Venice, her arms wrapped around Guy. "You found me."

Guy still could not speak. He shook his blue streak at Venice, as if it were a bouquet.

"Look at you—is that for me?"

"Do you like it? Is it okay?"

"Mmmmmm. I love it. I want it."

"Really?"

"I got you something."

"What?"

"This," said Venice, and she leaned in for another kiss.

"Ohhhh," Guy moaned.

"Darling, we've got to scoot. We've got to go everywhere."

Then Venice took a ferocious bite out of Guy's streak.

"You are delicious," she remarked.

Guy was unable to resist his wife's behavior, although she exhausted him only a bit less than she excited him. Venice took Guy's hand, and they were off.

The coatcheck was impossible, as Hassad roared after six white minks and Lucy's bottle-green princess coat with velvet collar and matching skating muff. The coatcheck girls ignored everyone and continued their phone conversations.

"Excuse me," said the first coatcheck girl, to the line of check-bearers, "I'm on the phone. I'm *busy.*"

"Christ," said the second coatcheck girl. "These people."

"Oh, Oded," sighed Lucy, amid the tumult, "it's been fun."

"You are being the bad mama jama," cooed Fadood, salivating over the epic span of Lucy's shoulders, which in his homeland might fetch three cabbages, a ladle and a barely used prayer rug.

"I am wanting to be more with the dancing," moaned Salima.

"And with the drinking," said Ramira.

"And with the shirtless ones," said Hofstra.

"And with the whiteness of the pleasure in the nose," added Tira, to a palm.

"Wives," murmured Hassad. "We are to be making the chosen of Fadood welcome in the tent."

The wives' sunglasses shook with indignation. They turned and spat on Lucy Yates Membrane, and Fadood's little goat butted her knees. The crack of Hassad's whip echoed in the lobby. Respect was restored.

"Oh please," said Licky Banes. "How last year."

Guy and Venice cleared the front door of the Club. The crowd in the street was cheering.

"My dears, you missed everything!" said Licky Banes, who had preceded the couple. "It was positively violent! These three people in, what can I say, pure petroleum products, well they simply charged the boy on the door! One broke his arm, the other kissed him, and the little one bit him on the leg! It was fabulous, my dears, it was television!"

The Club's bouncers had made short work of Bruce, Debbie and Michelle. No one was sure if the Jerseyans were still alive.

The wail of an ambulance drew near. The medics had been called to collect the injured door.

Among the elite, a "doorman" is someone who tends the entrance to an apartment building, in maroon twill, gold braid and cap. The eye that governs a nightspot's entry is known as a "door." The "doorman" enjoys dignity, a pension and grandchildren; the "door" makes do with omnipotence. The "door" is the humble pivot on which Manhattan nightlife turns. And now a door was bleeding.

Venice comforted this door, who stared up at her with gallant eyes. "It's all right . . ." he choked, "they didn't get in."

"Don't worry about a thing," Venice said. "Just look at me."

"Gee, are you okay?" Guy asked the door. "Do you want some gum?"

"They should take him to First Presbyterian," said someone in the crowd. "New sound system."

"Please," said Licky Banes, "but no. Manhattan General, there's a cancer wing—*they* get heroin!"

"I like Eye and Ear, on Sixty-fifth," offered Lucy, "the Membrane Pavilion, use my name, I'm sure there won't be a problem."

"Darling, can we hop in with you?" Venice asked the ambulance driver. "There's such a crush, the cabs can't get through, you're a dream. Guy, squeeze right in near that tank."

Guy had never been in an ambulance before. "Boy, is this oxygen?" he asked, pulling a plastic mask over his nose. "Whooooa!"

"Fabulous," said Venice, who inhaled, then passed the mask to the wounded door, as the ambulance nosed through the crowd and into the street.

"Darling, we're going downtown," Venice called to the driver. "A detour, we're too awful."

Guy and Venice settled in behind a folded wheelchair, girding themselves with pillows as the ambulance picked up speed. They tried to be good, given their surroundings, but they had been apart for hours. The ambulance was surprisingly cozy, a hayride. Before long the Hubers discovered the tongue depressors and the stethoscope. Soon they'd toppled to the ambulance's floor, elevating limbs and administering alcohol rubs.

"Hey, ya hear da one about da two dagos, walkin' into a open manhole?" the driver asked.

Venice looked into the rearview mirror and gave the driver a steamy glance.

"I love you," she mouthed to the driver.

That was when they went smack into the side of a crosstown bus. The radio still worked, so no one minded. By the time the ambulance got moving again, Guy and Venice had lost only an hour, so they could still make a night of it.

2

Good Afternoon

Guy and Venice wound up keeping the ambulance until dawn; the convenience was extraordinary. The Hubers decided to delay their honeymoon, as there was so much to do in town. The ambulance driver dropped the couple at their home, just a little after 11 a.m. The Hubers wanted to turn in early, as it was a weeknight.

Guy was not sure exactly which weeknight. He did not work, so the days would blur. Monday was easy to spot, as everyone was cranky, except Guy. If everyone was wearing a slap more cologne than usual, it was probably Friday, and Sunday was always tedious. Most people welcome Sunday, as a day of rest, but Guy never had anything to rest from. Guy feared Sundays, when boredom would invade every pore. He would pace and twitch, certain the phone must be out of order. On Sundays Guy would long for death, because at least it would be something to do.

Guy and Venice lived in a loft "the size of a football field," as the realtor had chanted. The loft occupied the top floor of a downtown building; decades earlier the space had housed millinery equipment and child laborers. Three sides of the loft were windowed, and there were a few columns; otherwise there was nothing but ozone, air by the bolt, an enviable urban heaven.

Guy liked his loft because he could close his eyes, stretch out his arms and whirl around, without bumping into anything. He could dance wildly, as if on an open plain; the loft encouraged grand gestures. Sometimes Guy and Venice would pull on heavy wool socks, and, after a running start, slide up and down the length of their home, as if they were surfing. The loft had more practical benefits as well. Guy could make a mess, and then another, and the loft would still appear relatively tidy, the wreckage swallowed by the scale.

The walls of the loft were painted white, and the floor was a slick mesa of blond wood. There was an enclosed bedroom and a kitchen area, and almost no furniture. Guy had never gotten around to choosing anything. Decorating trends came and went so quickly that he found it more relaxing to remain uncommitted. Venice's arrival two weeks earlier had lent the premises more of an identity, that of a mammoth attic.

Venice had spotted an intricately carved Black Forest mirror at the demolition of a hotel lobby. Guy had hauled the mirror home and leaned it against a wall. The couple had found two additional treasures at a junk sale. The first was a top-loading Coca-Cola refrigeration unit, the sort of thing used in pool halls or stadiums, a rounded chunk of tin with the familiar red and white logo. The unit no longer chilled, so Guy and Venice used the refrigeration wells to store sweaters. The second find was a deep green steamer trunk. It was a magical trunk, plastered with decals from long dry-docked cruise ships and world capitals now hopelessly Communist; it was fitted with quilted drawers and satin pockets. Guy and Venice had opened the trunk and stood it on end near the center of the loft. They would pretend they were packing their summer things, their tennis togs and picture hats, for the Lido. Venice's fashion magazines, from any of twelve nations, were stacked everywhere, a miniature skyline of print. When Guy and Venice had people at the loft, they would apologize profusely for the disarray and lack of seating, but guests always had a fine time. Visitors would float through the whiteness, murmuring, elements in a post-industrial Magritte. "You don't need furniture," Venice had concluded, "if you use enough blush."

Guy and Venice bounced into their loft this particular morning, giddy from an evening spent together, just the two of them and the city of New York. They couldn't remember all the places they'd been, or whom they'd seen, or what they'd done, but it didn't matter. They were home now. Entering the bedroom, they savored that delectable, gawky pause known only to new lovers, that hesitant, polite recess before lovemaking. Should we chat? Exchange childhood injustices? Indicate a maturity and a control to our relationship?

"I had a great night," said Guy, trying to be a gentleman.

"Get over here," Venice replied, standing on the bed.

That was the last thing Guy could remember, except for a blinding white light and the face of God.

At two in the afternoon, a lunatic jimmied the building's security system and rode the freight elevator to the Hubers' floor. Dance music blared from the street radio that swayed on the trespasser's shoulder, a radio that was more luggage than machine. The man stood outside the Hubers' door and pressed their buzzer insistently.

Guy dragged himself from the bedroom. He flinched at the virulent sunshine streaming through the many windows. Luckily, Guy had fallen asleep with his sunglasses still in place, so he didn't stumble. Except for the glasses, Guy was naked. He

peered through the peephole in the loft's steel entry slab to find
that the intruder had placed his open mouth over the hole from
the other side. Could this be a murderer? Guy wondered. A cat
burglar? An addict, or somebody who had escaped from something? Why would such a person suck on his door?

Impressed, Guy groggily released the slab. There stood Licky
Banes, lips akimbo, with radio, a Mammy red bandana bloused
over his head and a feather duster stuck in his rear pocket.

"Hi, Licky," said Guy, through a haze. "What's up?"

Licky strode past Guy and deposited himself atop the steamer
trunk, crossing his legs, like a starlet awaiting photographers
on a pier. He loosened his sneakers and declared, "Darling,
don't you know? Venice hired me—I'm the new maid."

Guy, more than satisfied, returned to bed. Venice hadn't mentioned hiring Licky, but Guy didn't mind. A maid was perfect
for newlyweds. Venice always had the best ideas. Guy kissed
the back of his wife's neck, and fainted.

Licky busied himself with Venice's magazines—who can resist a fresh horde? *Glaze* was Licky's favorite monthly, defini-
tive eye candy. If *Glaze* covered a famine, the pages would trum-
pet, "Waistlines Are Back!" Caronia Desti, the magazine's
editrix, had once been told of man's first steps on the moon.
"Zero gravity!" she had exclaimed. "I see scarves!"

Licky soon exhausted the back issues and headed for the bedroom. Guy and Venice's bedroom was as bare as the rest of the
loft, except for the bed—a wide mattress set on a plywood plat-
form—and the clothes. Clothes were heaped in blobby Alpine
ranges; clothes were hung on hooks and nails and open doors;
clothes were draped across Guy and Venice's sleeping figures.
There were iron pipes hung from chains, outlining the room
at eye level, and a second series above that; these pipes over-
flowed with hanging garments, plastic dry-cleaning sacks puck-
ering every few feet. The bedroom seemed in motion, battling
a tornado of fashion, an army of outfits unwilling to settle in

rows and drawers. The clothes were curiously threatening, as if at any moment a blouse or jacket might descend and whip itself around an unwary visitor.

Guy was reawakened by an evening dress swatting him in the face. Licky was rifling Venice's racks, with the keen eye of a Wichita librarian searching out pornography to ban and take home.

"You know," said Licky, considering a cocktail veil, "Venice hasn't a thing to wear. *Temps perdu,* my dears, *temps perdu.*"

"Licky," Guy groaned, trying to sleep, "are you really the maid?"

"But yes," said Licky, astonished in a fetching tulle boa, "of course. You need me. Venice and I are exactly the same size."

Licky had been asked to leave his last address, the penthouse of a publishing magnate, earlier that day. The magnate's wife had been late for a facial peel and had asked Licky, as the family governess, to explain the facts of life to her eight-year-old son. Licky had done just that.

"They may have canned me," Licky told Guy, "but that child will be able to have any man he wants. Thank God I had just enough time to get through annulments, choosing a silver pattern, and the gag reflex. I swear, sometimes I just don't understand people."

What is Licky's problem? Why does he say these things? To annoy, to shock, to upset? Not especially—Licky's speech pattern was innate, wholly unconscious, the italics, the filth, the exaggeration as effortless as an infant's gurgle. Licky had pledged a lifelong vow of chatter as surely as Trappists choose silence. Silence was Licky's sworn foe; he despised dead air as a decorator abhors an empty room. Licky's babble ornamented the atmosphere, spinning curlicues and tassels, forcing out the ordinary, the flat, the numbingly wholesome. Licky was naturally artificial, a diamond preferring to be rhinestone. Were Licky's more internal organs removed, he would live; were his tongue to be severed, even under careful anesthesia, he would expire at once.

At loose ends, Licky had settled on the Hubers. (He would later tell Venice that Guy had hired him.) Licky insisted on living as a member of the servant class; no one could accuse him of climbing, and he could cultivate an appropriate shiftlessness. Like any modern domestic, Licky considered himself less an employee than an honored houseguest.

"You're plain, decent folk," Licky told the comatose Hubers. "Hot but not pushy. Rich but underfurnished. Drugged but aware. If you were Italian, nineteen, and six foot three, I would marry you. Hush, darling," he cautioned himself, "remember your place." And then, ruefully, to Guy and Venice, "I load sixteen tons, and *what* do I get?"

"Vittorio?" murmured Venice, turning woozily in bed. "Darling, I've got to run. Oh Vittorio, calm down . . ." And then she promptly fell back asleep.

Time passed, and soon Danilo, the Hubers' dog, was wearing all of Venice's jewelry. Danilo was a coal black Akita, a vague sphere of pedigreed fuzz, the very latest canine. Once people had owned poodles; the beagle had ruled a reactionary era; and the Shih Tzu, Pekinese and Lhasa had all spent a moment in the sun, and the park. No one knew what became of these animals when their vogues had ceased. Were they farmed out to the suburbs, along with other discarded rages; were they pushed to the back of the bureau, with the hula hoops and mood rings and pogos?

Danilo was an ideal pet for Guy and Venice. Like his owners, he resisted exercise, spending his day rapt before the Black Forest mirror. He would rest on his haunches, his tiny black eyes squinting anxiously—for what? Acne? Crow's-feet? Fleas? Danilo could not be walked for any extended period of time, as he collapsed. Danilo was in high demand for breeding purposes, but Guy and Venice had not yet found time to meet his prospective bitches and get to know them, as dogs.

Licky, bored to tears, dropped a half-eaten box of Lucerne truffles onto Guy and Venice and allowed the dog to rouse the couple in pursuit of the candy.

"Jon?" mumbled Venice, almost pulling herself up on a lovely elbow.

"Venice, get up," said Licky, planting himself languidly on a corner of the bed. "You look awful."

"*Jon,*" said Venice, as the dog greedily licked her face, "that's disgusting . . . of course I do . . ."

"Guy, get up," Licky insisted. "We've got to get out of here, this place is a wreck."

"But Licky," Guy moaned, burrowing under his pillow, "you're the maid."

"Darling, I know," Licky replied, "I just called a service; they'll be here any minute, they'll do everything. I gave them your charge number." Really, thought Licky, I only have two hands. I wish I had more . . .

"Gee, a service?" Guy asked, confused.

"Darling, don't tell me how to do my job."

Eventually Guy and Venice got up and stumbled to the bathroom. The loft's architect had concentrated his resources on this room, so it was really the nicest spot on the block. Completely tiled in imported porcelain, the bathroom was a spa, a capsule, a gleaming ode to sybaritic cleanliness. There was a raised tub in the center of the room, with a whirlpool. Venice filled the tub with suds and slid in. Venice adored the tub, it felt sinfully immense, proportioned for asses' milk and handmaidens. Venice lay back, submerged to her chin. "Hello, darlings," she told her many beauty preparations aligned at the tub's edge, "I'm ready."

A shower stood nearby, sheathed in glass bricks. Jets of soothingly temperate water were pulsed at every orifice of the body within. Guy had not taken many showers in college; it had not been the thing to do. But lately, he could laze beneath the spray for hours in an exuberant baptism. A long shower approached sleep, and the womb itself. Guy lathered himself with a terrycloth bath mitt shaped like a giraffe.

There was music in the bathroom, streaming from artfully concealed speakers. Guy and Venice required melody at all times, as a soundtrack, a score. The couple never really stopped dancing, they scrubbed, gargled and moisturized to the beat. Music heightens life, even the most mundane aspects turn celebratory. Guy tried not to look at Venice while they bathed—the bathroom was too sexy, if they started something, they might drown. Outsize bathrooms are the only true decadence.

"I love soap . . ." Venice murmured, her head thrown back, as she disappeared beneath her bubbles.

After their bathroom epiphany, Guy and Venice were tempted to return to bed, but they did not. In robes and towel turbans, they padded toward the kitchen area, at Licky's request.

Licky had prepared a meal in the center of the loft. Each place was set with a sumo still life: a paper towel, chopsticks and a long-playing record, the last with a glowing blue pill placed at the center. Licky loved to cook.

"Darling, what are these?" asked Venice, swallowing her pill.

"Brunch," said Licky.

"They're really pretty," said Guy, downing his. "They look kind of familiar."

"Really?" said Licky. "They were in this plastic bottle in the corner; the label said Dr. Flaxman."

"Flaxman?" said Venice. "Bob Flaxman? With the eyes? Isn't he Danilo's veterinarian?"

"Gee, that's right," said Guy. "Remember, we were supposed to give him these when he had worms."

"Sweethearts, I'm sorry," said Licky, grimacing. "Health food."

Guy, still hungry, heated a croissant in the microwave oven. Guy worshipped the microwave, as superstitious tribesmen honor the bicycle pump or cap pistol. The microwave ejects brownies in seconds, banquets in less. Guy was certain the microwave operated on voodoo, materializing food from another dimension, snatching snacks from a galactic pastry warp.

Guy's croissant turned out to be a ceramic pin box in the shape of a croissant, which someone had given Venice as a party favor. Guy was forced to finish the chocolate truffles.

"Guy, we need food," said Venice, inspecting the refrigerator, which contained makeup, penicillin and a pair of handcuffs.

"And I need my first paycheck," said Licky, "and your deposit."

To stress his point, Licky drew a smile face in the thick dust on the refrigerator door.

"We need bucks," said Guy thoughtfully, drying his hair. "Let's go see my parents!"

Everyone then got dressed, which took forever, as everyone needed at least two mirrors, so they could see how they looked from the back. Guy wore yesterday's outfit, because it was on the top of the pile where he'd tossed it. Although Guy loved the scent of freshly washed clothes, doing laundry posed a Herculean task. Guy had been raised in a home where the help did the wash, returning it in bright, lemon-freshened, neatly folded stacks. Guy would press these stacks to his face; there is nothing quite like wash, that incomparable detergent high. Guy unconsciously assumed that those obliging Jamaican women were still around, ironing and matching socks and picking his things up off the floor.

Guy knew this was untrue, and the condition of his clothing sometimes appalled him. Vowing to improve, he would pack everything into a pillowcase and head for the laundromat. About halfway there, he would remember that he never knew when to add the bleach. Then he would find a garbage pail and throw everything out.

I guess I have a fear of laundry, Guy decided, slipping into his T-shirt. He found a thin iridescent black necktie on a doorknob and knotted it around his bare neck. He was going to Park Avenue, after all. Then he put on his biker's jacket and hung a crucifix from his ear. Guy shunned violence, except as an exercise in style. Guy had never been in a fight. During his childhood, his aggressive impulses had been channeled into work with modeling clay and sessions with the school psychologist. Guy even had trouble at scary movies; he would sink into his seat, keeping his eyes squinched shut until he heard the chainsaw stop.

Guy looked at himself in the mirror. There always seemed to be a halo about him, a rosy, aureate softness which spoke of housekeepers neatly clipping his sandwich crusts and doting hands forever wiping his mouth.

Boy, I'm such a spaz, Guy thought; I want to be a killer! He arranged his terminal blacks and ragged leather and attempted a Brando arrogance, with Belmondo lips. If he stood very still and held his breath, he almost had it. Then Venice and Licky started applauding, and the effect fell to pieces.

"You guys," said Guy sheepishly. "Stop! I looked so good! I'm going to get a tattoo!"

"My dear, of what?" Licky asked. "And where?"

"Well," said Guy, trying to think. "I could get a dragon, or like a heart, with a dagger, that says 'Born to Raise Hell.' I could get it on my arm, but, gee, then my parents would kill me, or I could get it on my chest, but that probably really hurts."

"I'll do it," said Venice. She picked up a ballpoint pen and moved toward Guy. "I'll just heat this up."

"No!" said Guy. "Then I'll get ink poisoning! You guys! Come on, don't you think I look lean and mean?"

"And keen," Licky answered, ending the controversy.

"Is this all right?" asked Venice, studying herself in the mirror. She had tugged an oversize sweatshirt over her naked flesh. "Is it too much?"

"Yes," said Licky.

"Good," said Venice, pulling at her neckline.

"It's chilly," Guy warned.

"It's sable," Venice decided. She put on her calf-length fur, arranging it to slouch over her shoulders. She added a pair of white canvas deck shoes and she was done. The difference between Venice dressed and Venice nude was a fine line. If the truth were known, makeup was Venice's first love. Once her eyes were on, she had to be reminded to get dressed or she might well leave the house wearing little else.

"Licky, that's a great sweater," said Guy. "Is it mine?"

"Darling, I need a uniform," said Licky, admiring himself in a black lambswool cableknit. "Talk to my union."

"Let's go," said Venice. "I'm boiling."

Guy, Venice and Licky looked at one another and nodded. They were ready to face the world. As one, they gave a rebel yell, a raucous Yee-HA! as football squads do after a huddle. Then they all held their heads, as it was still awfully early in the day for yelling.

3

En Route

Guy, Venice and Licky left the building, stepping out into the late afternoon. Venice slipped her arm into Guy's; he went weak whenever Venice did this. The gesture seemed more intimate than sex. Guy pictured himself ice-skating, his hands linked with his wife's, the two of them gliding through life.

Licky jumped to the curb and extended his arm in the familiar hailing signal, the Manhattan salute. Licky believed that cabs improved any trip a thousandfold. The mere sight of a taxi cheered Licky immensely, he felt every cab was sent just for him by his mother. At the moment, however, the cabs were decidedly unfeeling, all either full or flashing a cruel OFF-DUTY beacon. Licky bowed to Venice, who left Guy and ambled into the street, her sable draped to her waist.

An off-duty cab immediately slowed for a better look, and Venice leaned forward as the driver rolled down his window.

"Darling, are you free?" Venice asked, staring into the driver's eyes.

"Sure, toots," the driver leered.

"Good," said Venice, as Guy and Licky piled into the back of the cab.

"Hey, who are those guys?" the driver asked, as Venice climbed in beside Guy.

"Darling, really," said Venice, scolding. "This is my husband, and that's my maid."

"We love your cab," said Licky.

Guy gave the driver his parents' address, and everyone settled in.

"Well, my dears," said Licky, igniting the day's gossip, "Jon Gelle went home with Ratallia, too terribly touching, although I personally find her too lesbian for words."

Licky had been finding many people too lesbian for words lately, and no one was quite sure why.

"She's a whore," said Venice, as a compliment, "but she's never with women. Is she?"

"Darling, being too lesbian is a spiritual quality. Now, I adore lesbians, I could squeeze them by the hour, but they're, well, *practical. Earth*bound. *Hide*bound. *Alabama* bound. Too lesbian for words!"

"What about Lucy?" asked Guy. "Is she a lesbian?"

"Don't start," said Licky. "That one's the absolute *thesaurus* of human sexuality, we must find *new words* for her potential—did she go off with that Arab?"

Venice was about to reply, but she was distracted. The cab had stopped for a light, and she peered out the window. There was a mob gathered at a storefront, people chatting and primping, as if they were outside a nightspot. Venice thought she recognized a face, but she wasn't sure.

"Darling," said Venice, interrupting Licky's news update, "that man over there, going into that place—is that Carl Gambon?"

"Of course, darling," said Licky, hanging out the window.

"Hi, Carl! Look at him, with those gray temples and a pocket square. And *look* where he's going! Ooo-la-la!"

"Darlings, I've got to hop," said Venice. She kissed Guy, firmly, so he would remain kissed during her absence. "Guy, tell your parents I love them, but I had to go. Will I see you tonight?"

"Tonight?" said Guy, dazed, still recovering from the kiss. "At de?"

"But jais," said Venice, using a current Hungarian slang. "Do you love me?"

"Yes!" said Guy, stricken at any possible doubt.

"Oooooh," Venice pouted, kissing Guy's nose. "Lucky you. Bye!"

The cab sped off, leaving Venice on the sidewalk. The storefront was a woebegone affair, a ghostly bodega reclaimed by the city. Yet the crowd multiplied. Venice waved to friends as she picked her way through the broken glass and ruptured cement.

No one noticed the debris, as the storefront contained Manhattan's preeminent welfare clinic, famed for its lightning-quick venereal testing. People could go to private doctors, but the results took forever and the music in the waiting room was always awful. The storefront was more chummy, more gala, and patients always ran into someone they knew. The clinic was a sex clubhouse, a canteen, where hard-boiled veterans could gather and swap war stories as they were readied for a return to the trenches. There was a distinct romance to the clinic, a wartime equality. The wounded would stagger in, and everyone would slap them on the back, as if they'd been shot down over the Somme.

By the time Venice reached the door, Carl Gambon, an attaché at the Luxembourg Embassy, had already entered the clinic. Venice was not sure if she had slept with Monsieur Gambon, but there was a chance, and syphilis was no laughing matter, unless listed as the object of one of Caronia Desti's legendary scavenger hunts.

Venice scanned the clinic, with its charred walls and mottled linoleum. Flyblown placards were taped here and there. One placard featured a wicked Oriental woman, with long finger-nails, in a tight sheath. The caption read, "Beware The Good-Time Gal." *Great* dress, Venice thought.

Carl Gambon was sitting beside an infested pimp. Venice strode over. "Carl," she said, standing before the sporty diplo-mat, her hands on her hips.

"Venice!" said Carl. "Don't worry, I'm just in for shots. I'm being sent to Belgium; it's absolute hell."

"Poor baby," said Venice, relieved.

"Will you come with me?" Carl begged. "Why won't you take my calls? Why are you torturing me?"

"Oh, Carl," Venice sighed, "don't be too lesbian for words!"

"Venice, I adore you!"

"Darling, I'm married," Venice said, sternly.

"You're married?" said Carl, incredulously. "You?"

"But jais," Venice said, marveling, "I'm an old married lady. Almost a week. It's fabulous."

Venice held up her cigarette. Carl reached for his lighter, but had a better idea. He pulled out a shiny new key and held it up.

"Yes?" said Venice.

"It's my Jaguar," said Carl. "It's yours. Please."

"*Carl,*" said Venice, still waiting for a light.

"Come to Belgium. I have a villa, you'll adore it. Don't tell your husband, don't even pack, I'll buy you all new things."

Venice took Carl's key. She handed it to the welfare mother in the next seat.

"Here, darling," Venice said to the woman.

"*¿Como?*" said the woman, a plump lady surrounded by neatly dressed children busy with coloring books.

"Someone's got to take it," Venice told the woman. "It's only a Jag, but what can you do? Don't go to Belgium."

Carl Gambon began spluttering furiously, and tried to retrieve his key from the welfare mother.

"¡Vaya! No me molesta, pendejo!" the welfare mother warned, and her children looked up. The three-year-old stared daggers at Monsieur Gambon and broke her crayon, ominously.

"I'm married," Venice told the woman joyfully. "Could you die?"

"And Tanzo, well my dear," Licky continued, in the taxi, "it's been confirmed. Everything you've heard is true, he is a necrophiliac."

"Wait," said Guy. "You mean, he likes to do it with dead people? I mean, dead dead people?"

"Of course," said Licky, "I'm sure if they're wiggling even the teeniest bit it just ruins it for him. I mean, the date would be off."

"Wow," said Guy. "That's so weird. But wait, where does he get them? I mean, the dead bodies?"

"Oh darling, please," said Licky. "The city morgue. Everybody knows that; it's a madhouse down there. On Friday nights you can't get near the place."

"Boy," said Guy, "I'm so out of it. Licky, how do you know all this stuff?"

"Please," protested Licky, "it's all common knowledge. I mean, ask anyone. You can't not hear these things. I mean, I'm an American. Oh my God."

Licky always kept an eye on the boulevard as he gossiped; he never wanted to miss a trick. Now he shot out the window, to the waist, his eyes wide.

"What?" asked Guy, grabbing Licky's ankles to prevent an accident. "What is it?"

"STOP!!!!" Licky screamed, and the cab ground to a halt,

skidding against a lamppost and narrowly missing a mailman, all things the driver enjoyed doing.

"Licky, are you all right?" Guy asked, terribly worried.

"Darling," said Licky, clutching his chest, and fanning himself furiously with his other hand, as a geisha might. *"Behold!"*

There was a construction site directly opposite the cab. Standing beside a portable toilet shell was a muscular young man in a sweat-stained workshirt, workpants, a toolbelt, and a plastic hardhat.

"My husband," intoned Licky, leaving the cab. He wafted toward the puzzled young man, with the innocence of a cloud-borne ballerina in a dream sequence.

Licky often chose contact with the lower orders, out of a hunger for primitive combustion, labor-hardened thighs and miscellaneous swarthiness. Licky also preferred people with limited vocabularies, as they tended not to interrupt.

"Excuse me," said Licky to the young man, breathlessly, "are these bolts? Or *rivets?"*

Boy, thought Guy, alone in the cab, everyone's so busy today! It was never easy to hold a group together on a trip uptown, there was so much to look at, so many magnets and ambushes. If Eros didn't jab, the shop windows would beguile. If there was nothing in the stores, a marquee would tempt. I'll just tell my folks that Venice and Licky say hello, Guy decided. Guy caught his own eye roving toward a street vendor wheeling a cart laden with stuffed toy penguins. The penguins were plump plush angels, with yellow rubber beaks and top hats and jaded, rolling eyes. Stuffed toy penguins, Guy thought, they're so neat! I could buy one for Venice, and another just because they are so great, and—but I don't have any cash!

"Park Avenue," said Guy to the driver, cheerfully repeating his parents' address.

4

Park Avenue

The cab soon arrived at the Huber townhouse, on Park Avenue, an address of sumptuous repression. There are almost no shops on Park Avenue, and the flowers nurtured on the road medians are kept in rigid formation. The residents of Park Avenue have forbidden any lighting displays at Christmastime, with a handful of poinsettias allowed only as a sop to religious factions.

Guy secretly liked Park Avenue. When life grew too hectic he would visit, as if leaving town entirely. Park Avenue is a compound, where the sidewalks are always impeccably deserted, except for the sunning doormen and an occasional nanny and child. Park Avenue is a high gray corridor, a bastion of taste and stillness, an immaculate granite canyon where the garbage is sequestered in basement grottoes and whisked away in the dead of night, as if it had never existed; Hitchcock garbage.

The Huber townhouse was sandwiched between two mammoth apartment buildings. The townhouse had a stained limestone facade and appeared appropriately dour. The Hubers hoped the townhouse's humorless architecture would disguise the shameful source of the Huber fortune. The family lode was based in a domestic champagne.

Cordon Huber was available primarily in six-packs, and the vineyards bloomed in upstate New York. Guy's parents always hurried past liquor stores, where the latest vintage—also available in the popular gallon jug—could be found stacked in humiliating pyramids, beside a sweepstakes offer. The Hubers never served the home brew, and Guy remembered his mother stroking his forehead at bedtime and murmuring, "At least we're not a beer."

Considering that the only truly Old Money in America would have to exist in wampum and arrowheads, the Hubers put on a remarkable show of gentility. The townhouse displayed all the negligent hallmarks of true aristocracy, the car keys scratching the Queen Anne highboy, the ski boots strewn across the Aubusson. The colors were those dead greens and trying Wedgwood jaspers, set off by poor lighting and windows encrusted with what can only be called draperies. The Huber place was a fusion of boathouse and mausoleum, a setting in which one might tie flies or entertain a prime minister. As Mr. Huber put it, "A place just doesn't feel right until somebody's died there."

Guy arrived at dinnertime. He greeted the downstairs servants, who said, "Oh Mister Guy, now don't you look nice." Guy always felt slightly uncomfortable around the servants. They seemed unnervingly pleased to serve, to watch soap operas and eat cold cuts and put their children through medical school. Guy knew he should organize the servants, rabble-rouse, treat the cook to a Brecht revival; but Guy also knew that without servants, there would be no hors d'oeuvres with toothpicks and no shiny bathroom tile or nice smells. Servants were all that stood between man and chaos, or at least between man and Guy having to unload the dishwasher himself. He decided he would consult Licky on the issue. Licky definitely had perspective.

Guy skipped up the stairs to the dining room, swinging on the bannisters. He felt like he was visiting an historic re-creation of his childhood: here is the landing where Young Guy broke his ankle, and here is the umbrella stand where Young Guy used to hide the food he didn't like. He reached the dining room, where he had never spent much time. Guy and his broth-ers had always eaten in front of television, like enraptured chil-dren everywhere, watching their dessert being advertised.

"Hi, guys!" said Guy, bounding into the dining room, a proper chamber of wallpaper, wainscot and sideboards. Guy's father was seated at the head of the burnished mahogany table, enjoying his pheasant with mayonnaise. Mrs. Huber was con-templating the festive raffia placemats she had purchased on a recent trip to Guadalajara.

"Son," said Guy's father, looking up from his paper as Guy came in, "good to see you."

"Hello, dear," said Guy's mother, and, to her husband, "Look, dear, it's Guy."

Guy's father was a large, solid man who read the paper. He undoubtedly had a face, and personal habits, but he was not the sort of man who concerned himself with such matters. Guy's father did not work for the family business in any direct capac-ity. He did something else, perhaps law, or brokerage; Guy had never really understood. Fearing it might be boring, he had never made any inquiries. All Guy knew was that his father wore well-cut (but never showy) suits, hand-stitched English wingtips, and stately, inspiring topcoats, and that he did what-ever he did in a mahogany-paneled office, and that he took what-ever he did home at night in a superbly worn leather attaché.

Guy adored his father's stolidity, as an anchor in a far too lively universe. As long as Mr. Huber remained distant and un-ruffled, Guy knew he would not be drafted. Guy did not intend to emulate his father, but he appreciated him; he felt lucky. Guy counted on his father to always ask him how school was, even though Guy had graduated more than two years back. Guy's father was such a *Dad*.

Guy's mother was a busy woman, able to lead a full, even a robust life without losing her knack for stunningly careless floral arrangements. Mrs. Huber had a pale, distracted look, as if she were always trying to recall just how many oyster plates the maid had shattered. Mrs. Huber's hair was prematurely silver, with a yellowish cast; golf and sun and weeding had conspired to make Mrs. Huber appear older than her mate, the lot of so many Protestant wives.

Mrs. Huber had raised Guy and his two brothers (both doing well, one in academia and the other in small arms sales to Gambia). Then she had decided to become a person. Becoming a person entailed mostly course work in Persian Enamels. In addition, Mrs. Huber was employed two half-days per week at The Manhattan Museum of Larger Art. Her duties at the museum included compiling the illustrations for the annual datebooks, so she combed the collections for any work with a cat in it.

Mrs. Huber wore classic grays and navies, with a searing hot pink for special occasions. She was perhaps the last woman in Manhattan to wear a small pin, a circle or vermeil leaf, without irony. Guy felt protective toward his mother. He had once glimpsed her wandering into traffic while planning a menu on the back of an envelope. There had been a collision, the drivers cursing and bloody. Mrs. Huber had not noticed and had moved on, pausing to admire a trivet in a shop window. Guy found his mother's damask serenity both soothing and uncanny. It disturbed him only in its startling resemblance to the habits of Lucy Yates Membrane.

Guy never had any personal conversations with his parents and therefore loved them dearly. His love was returned in kind. A total lack of communication is the root of any happy family.

Guy entered the dining room, and everything seemed just

right. The tureen was in place, the pewter sconces were lit, and the good silver was safely tucked away in chamois bags in the wall safe.

"You guys look great," said Guy, patting his father's shoulder. "What's up?"

"Well, there seems to be a five-year-old girl, in Peru, who's given birth," said Guy's father. "Right here in the paper."

"Should we send something?" asked Guy's mother, who had never been seen eating. "We sent the Bemisses' girl a lovely serving piece; she sent such a nice note. Are they registered?"

"It doesn't say, Alice," answered Guy's father. "What a nuisance. And here's another fellow, out in Des Moines; he's eaten a car. Chopped it up, ate it, and not a single side effect, he's happy as the day he was born."

"Was it an American car?" asked Guy's mother. "They're really much nicer. I don't trust those Italian creations, with the young women inside, in buckets or something. I imagine they'd be very bad for you. Spicy."

"Well, there's a picture here; it seems to be a Ford wagon."

"Sensible. Guy, dear, come sit down, you look interesting. I was just telling Liz Woodyardle the other day, our Guy always looks interesting. Of course, Liz's boy, the youngest, he's still in that ashram, with his Perfect Master, he was on the street the other day, in peach chiffon, his head completely shaved, sores everywhere. I said, 'You see, Liz, your boy's interesting too.' "

"Hi, Mom," said Guy, kissing her on the cheek. A Mom cannot function until she has been kissed on the cheek, that kiss is a receipt for her years of selflessness. "How's the Museum?" Guy asked.

"It's fine, dear, really splendid, you know, we've got our big do coming up tomorrow; I understand Mrs. Desti is coming. And just last week, I found a lovely piece, a mummified kitten, preserved in all that muck at Pompeii. We've called her Mittens, and she'll be July in the new book."

"That's great, Mom," said Guy. "Uhm, can I talk to you guys about something?"

Mr. Huber put his paper down, something he had not done since Guy's conception.

"Certainly, dear," said Mrs. Huber, lowering her empty fork. "Is it these placemats? Are they too much?"

"Is it school, son?" asked Mr. Huber. "Sophomore Slump?"

"No," said Guy. "I mean, not exactly."

Guy took a deep breath. He hated asking his parents for money. Usually he just went to the bank, where his inheritance arrived in tasty monthly chunks. But this month had been expensive, with the wedding and all, and a bank officer had called the previous day. Guy was overdrawn, the officer had reported, and the bank deemed an advance out of the question.

Guy never kept a record of his checks; accounting struck him as desperately unromantic. Guy also did not own a wallet, as the bulge ruined the line of any decently snug pair of pants. He would just grab a batch of bills and fill his pockets, mashing the currency with ticket stubs, sticks of gum and house keys. Guy tried to be responsible about money; he longed to know the value of a dollar, but things just got away from him.

"It's nothing really," said Guy, plunging ahead. "I'm just all overdrawn on my trust, and the bank guys won't give me anything until next month, isn't that weird? And Licky needs a deposit, and there isn't any food, and I saw this great pair of shoes downtown, real zebra, they're amazing! Just a few bucks."

"Guy," said Mr. Huber, "this is very upsetting."

"Oh, no, don't worry, they made them a long time ago, before you weren't supposed to kill zebras, you know, like old dead zebras."

Guy knew the zebra shoes would persuade his parents; the shoes were ethereal. Pointed toes, side laces, a modified Cuban heel, and those primal stripes. Guy would almost be afraid to wear such perfection. Maybe he would just keep the shoes in their box, and look at them, the way art collectors visit their Leonardo sketch in the vault. Zebra shoes—this was beyond wrangling, beyond niggling debate. How could his parents refuse?

"Dear," said Mrs. Huber, "what your father means is, we're concerned about the money question. Have you spent your Christmas things?"

"Mom," Guy explained patiently, "I had to get my hair cut."

"Son," said Mr. Huber, "when I was your age, I'd learned to manage my money. What about your investments?"

"Well," said Guy, trying to remember, "I have fifty dollars put down on a jukebox, it's a 'Maestro, Please' from the Forties—the guy at the store said it was really unusual, 'cause of the bubble panels. And I went to a benefit thing for this performance group that does silent opera, it was tax deductible, and, uhm . . . oh, I bought a ginseng root; if I leave it in a drawer for, like, ten years, it's supposed to be terrific! Does that count?"

"Dear," said Mrs. Huber, "I think it's time we had a talk."

The remainder of the family's conversation included sections on maturity, making practical use of one's fine education, Those Less Fortunate, and Life. Guy's father discovered that Guy no longer went to college, lending a cosmic gravity to matters. Mr. Huber's distress prompted him to share several pointed anecdotes about the formative July and August he'd spent at Guy's great-grandfather's vineyard, outside of Albany, overseeing the development of a pink champagne and presiding at tourist tastings. Guy's mother sobbed a bit, shook her head and spoke of the family going to hell in a handbasket, which even Mr. Huber felt was a tad strong. Guy kept notably silent, trying to come up with a suitably adult, participatory facial expression and a responsible tilt of the head.

Guy never knew what to do at a lecture. At school he would have fallen asleep or doodled, but neither seemed advisable at home. Guy's parents were looking right at him, and they were using that overly distinct, almost phonetic phrasing that parents resort to in time of crisis. Guy pictured himself in a laboratory cage, as two white-jacketed scientists attempted to establish a rapport. Guy half expected his mother to grab his palm and tap out the deaf alphabet for "water" or "not one penny." Guy wanted to help, to reach out across the vast tundra of parent/child relations, but he wasn't sure what was being demanded of him. Should he thump the table to indicate "yes" or "no"? Should he mimic his captors' gestures? Would a winning smile be enough?

Guy loved his parents deeply, and he hated to upset them. Guy's parents loved their son and desired only his happiness. Alas, money can jar even the truest affections. Guy began to feel uneasy, for a stranger had come to the table and put the family at odds, prodding and pinching, whispering scandal into unguarded ears, overturning the gravy boat, and uncoupling the gravy train. Finally, the chat came to a head, and the unmentionable lay before the once pastoral clan, somewhere in between the Cartier cruet set and Mr. Huber's patient tabloid.

"Guy," said Mr. Huber, "I think it's high time you started looking for work."

"Dad, I'd love to," said Guy, in an eminently reasonable tone, "but it's just that I'm really busy."

"We realize that, dear," said Mrs. Huber, "but you're just going to have to find the time."

"Wait," said Guy, hoping feverishly that the entire evening was some sort of drug flashback or neural misbehavior, "you mean, like, just go out and have an interview or something?"

"And then go to work," said Mr. Huber, "at your job."

The Huber fortune could easily support any indolence Guy might choose to pursue. This insistence on employment was a Puritan quirk, an anachronism not unlike the matched Tang Dynasty sabers which hung in the Huber entry hall, or the fact that the most recent Huber generation was born with functional legs. Day labor provided Guy's parents with an acceptable response, when friends asked What The Boys Were Up To. The Hubers pitied those parents forced to shrug, or share a doctor's opinion, when the exploits of grown children entered the conversation. "Ethan is in California," or "Nan will be able to come home in the Fall." Those poor families. How can they face anyone? What do they put in the newsletter? Mostly, though, the Hubers liked their sons to work as an example to the help.

"It'll be fun," said Mrs. Huber, her hostess skills reasserting themselves at the edge of the abyss. "I work, and I'm having a marvelous time!"

"Son, we're proud of you," said Mr. Huber. "Get crackin'!"

Guy, dazed, nodded and reached for a water goblet.

"Look," said Mrs. Huber, doting. "Our Guy, all grown up."

"A man," said Mr. Huber.

When Guy regained consciousness, he was lying on a parlor sofa, a comfortable, overstuffed piece covered in a Schumacher ivy repeat on a bone background.

"Get them off me!" Guy screamed, feeling the vines at his throat.

"You're fine, son," said his father. "Just a little light-headed. A job'll clear that right up."

"Here, dear," said Mrs. Huber, offering a Hershey's Kiss from the fluted silver dish. "Better?"

"I'm . . . fine," said Guy, still a little woozy, and then he howled and rolled under the sofa. "It bit me!"

"It's origami, dear," said Mrs. Huber, retrieving the finely folded parchment owl which had fallen from a curio shelf onto Guy's head. "It's fascinating. You think someone's passing you a note, and it's actually three imperial swans devouring a lotus."

"I'm sorry," said Guy, emerging and pulling himself back onto the sofa, as if suddenly paraplegic. "I must've blacked out or something; gee, I guess I haven't been eating."

"You college boys," said Mr. Huber, lapsing. "Livin' on donuts and rotgut. Shenanigans!"

Guy was soon able to stand. He did not wish to cause his family further dismay; he wanted his parents to be proud of him and never worry. Assuming a brave face, Guy kissed his mother, shook his father's hand and complimented the Honduran woman on the dinner. Then, pocketing his mother's tiny "Bon Voyage" check, he fell down the stair and let himself out.

"Goodbye, dear," said Mrs. Huber, picking up her crewel (a projected series of pillow shams, featuring frogs dressed in scuba gear, chef's hats and madras golf skirts). "Good luck."

"Goodbye, son," said his father. "Study hard, and don't let the team down."

"He's a good boy," said Mrs. Huber, as the door closed behind her youngest, her bunny, her baby. "We had to be firm."

"Fine chap," said Mr. Huber. "Has he got a girl?"

"I don't know," said Mrs. Huber thoughtfully, tying off a French knot. Guy and Venice's wedding had occurred a week ago, and although the Hubers genuinely liked Venice, she was so unsuitable that her existence refused to take root in either Mr. or Mrs. Huber's brains.

"Alice, here's a woman in Maine, visited by a creature," said Mr. Huber, returning to his paper. "It seems to have made passionate love to her, taken her to an asteroid and then left her by the road."

"Where in Maine?" asked Mrs. Huber. "Rockport? Perhaps

she knows the Wieldings. I spoke with Laura just the other day, she was so sweet about our Christmas card. We've had so many comments, I've begun to think about next year. Dear, shall we look in the catalogue?"

"Why, Alice," said Mr. Huber. "Let's."

5

Job Hunting

Guy left his parents' home and wandered into the street. He was thoroughly shell-shocked; he touched his arms and legs, to make certain they were still in place. Guy felt stunned, molested; his soul hurtled beyond him, torn from his flesh.

Guy was not willfully spoiled, he was spoiled as a leaf is green, organically, tenderly. It had never occurred to him to hold a job. Any attempt at honest labor, or even decent posture, seemed heresy, the hand of man in direct conflict with the peace of God.

Guy looked up, as cars whizzed about him; he had no idea who he was, or where he was. Guy felt in his pockets, for identification, for some sense of self. His fingers brushed his mother's check. A check, Guy thought, a *check!* He almost wept; the check seemed a memento, a touching reminder of a life that was now thousands of years in the past. A check! Guy rubbed the paper against his face, yearningly.

Guy remembered when his father had first taught him to

write and endorse checks. Guy had been a toddler; his father had sat him down. "Son," Mr. Huber had said, "it's time you learned about cash flow."

Mr. Huber had spent hours with Guy, the father and son poring over a set of toy checks provided by the bank. Mr. Huber had guided Guy's tiny hand, having the boy practice zeroes, and learn that dizzy squiggle after the scripted figures, and master a clean rip from the pad. Guy's eyes brimmed, recalling that idyll.

If Guy had any aptitude, it was for sleep. Is there anywhere nectar so sweet as sleep? Guy could get all goony just thinking about sleep, about gusting cotton sheets, and woolly blankets, and pillows, chubby goosefeather clouds to stack and fall into.

Guy was an innately horizontal person. He could do anything lying down. He liked to eat off trays and use a remote control for the TV. Guy admired Victorian women, those wan invalids spread across divans. He had studied the ancient Romans, who reclined at all times, during feasts and at lyre recitals and in senate session.

Sleep seemed so right to Guy, but he knew that many did not share his passion. Guy wanted to be fair; he had investigated, rising before noon on at least one occasion. Awake at ten, Guy had felt profoundly dislocated; the sunshine had scorched his retinas, he hadn't known what to do with his hands. Guy was convinced that nothing of any importance had ever occurred in the a.m. Why schedule a speech, a mass, a revolution for eleven in the morning—who would come?

Guy was so good at sleep, employment seemed a jagged intrusion, an error, a mismatch. Guy never felt idle; his days were more than full—he had Venice, dancing and sleep, if anything, he was overbooked. A job just made no sense; a job would never take advantage of Guy's native abilities, of his gift. Guy was born to sleep.

Guy wandered sightlessly for hours. He trailed down the city's long avenues, across rusting bridges and perilous off-ramps and honking intersections. Ultimately, auto-response took hold, and Guy found himself outside the Club de. It was already late in the evening and the throng had gathered. Some-one new was on the door, but he recognized Guy's streak from the morning papers. Guy was waved into the Club, past the jeer-ing, pleading usuals and the nice couple from Minneapolis with their creaseless safari outfits, their loaded Kodaks and what ap-peared to be a sawed-off shotgun.

"Look at that one, Mavis," said the husband, as Guy loped into the Club. "Long face and all."

Mavis turned her aluminum folding chair to get a better look. "Oh, Huey," she told her husband, "he'll be fine. Cute as a bug's ear." Mavis adjusted her souvenir kerchief ("We Saw Expo '69") and took a sip of cider from the thermos. "Need a nip, hon?" she asked Huey.

"Don't mind if I do," said Huey, pulling out his collapsible travel cup. "Hope we get in, hon."

"I'm having a fine time right here," said Mavis.

Guy was still in a haze. He tried to smile at the coatcheck girls, but he kept his jacket.

"Guy looks kinda bummed," said the first coatcheck girl.

"*He's* bummed!" protested the second coatcheck girl, playing with her flip. "Look at my life. Split ends for days."

Guy moved into the body of the Club, where the evening was just beginning, as people circled the mezzanine, ogling the dance floor but still unsure. Everyone noticed Guy's depression; he was ordinarily such a cheery boy, a fan, a pleasure.

"Hey dude," called the bartenders, "what's the hassle?"

Guy tried to speak, but only hoarse, gurgling sounds emerged.

"Dude," said the bartenders, "cool out."

"Ju are sad?" asked Ratallia Parv, wetting her lips sympathetically.

"Jais," Guy rasped. I'm such a party poop, he thought. He hurried upstairs and headed for the men's lounge to make himself presentable. The lounge echoed Guy's despair. The walls were lined with that deep blue mirror, the kind they don't make anymore. This mirror can only be found at certain preserved soda fountains. The color is a bottomless, slightly absurd blue, the shade of a lake set before a castle, in a children's book.

Guy could lose himself in that blue, and it matched the color of his streak. Was it Guy's imagination, or had his streak begun to change its tint, in accord with his emotional state? Had his head become one of those glass swans filled with liquid that went yellow or emerald to indicate relative humidity and forecast rain?

"Darling," said Venice, as Guy walked into the men's lounge. She turned, her flesh shifting in her black leather corset.

Venice had been adjusting her makeup in an appreciative atmosphere. Men and women shared the facilities at the Club de. No one wanted to miss out on a smidgen of architecture or banter or illegal substance. Public bathrooms had become the new salons, where society convened; some people never left the john all night, staking out a central commode and holding court. Sharing the loo allowed both sexes a tremor of satanic naughtiness, of Freudian hell, of genital riot.

"It's a zoo tonight," said Venice. "The ladies' room is worse, because there's dancing." Then she bent at the waist, until her head almost hit her knees. With a sharp swinging motion, she returned to an upright position. This was how Venice did her hair.

"How do I look?" she asked. "That good?"

"Boy, you look . . . wonderful," said Guy, barely audible.

"Darling," said Venice, noticing how pale Guy had become, "is something wrong? Are my lips crooked?"

"No," said Guy, trying to sparkle. "Your lips are great. They're neat. They're . . ."

Venice added a sly mascara moustache to Guy's upper lip. "Darling," she said, "you look blue."

"Well," said Guy, hoisting himself up on a sink, "I went to see my parents."

"Oh, *no!*" came Licky's voice from a stall, followed by some discreet panting, as Licky was not alone.

"My darling," said Venice, as she finished her eyes, "what did those animals do to you?"

"Gee," said Guy, "I don't know. Nothing, really. I feel like such a baby, you know?"

Venice put her hands on Guy's shoulders, focusing on him. She peered out from beneath her tangle of bangs. She was wearing black leather opera gloves, to the elbow. She rubbed a smooth finger on Guy's neck. Guy shut his eyes and nuzzled the finger.

"Come on," said Venice, pulling the finger away, "spill."

By this time a crowd had gathered in the men's lounge, aware that human events were about to transpire and conceivably produce gossip.

"Well," said Guy, addressing the mob, "I just needed, you know, some money, just to tide things over, just for food and things, and, you know, shoes."

"Ah," sighed Caronia Desti, as the mob nodded to one another, in immediate understanding.

"And, so my Dad was reading the paper, and my Mom was being my Mom, and I just sort of mentioned it, you know, and they got really weird. Does anyone have a cigarette?"

Guy did not smoke. He had always wanted to, but he could never master inhaling. He would cough and sputter, and look silly. The cigarette, so carelessly hung off his lower lip, would tumble to his lap, or go out. Smoking was irrevocably cool, but, like handling money, it was beyond Guy. Smokers always seem like French spies in black turtlenecks; smoking was one of the few careers Guy had ever considered. Once every year, Guy would try again, to see if his smoking karma had improved.

The crowd in the men's lounge offered hundreds of brands. Guy chose an imported Roman label, black with a silver filter, and very becoming. Just to be safe, Guy decided not to light up.

"Your parents! Did they *strike* you?" moaned Licky, from his stall. "Ahhhhh . . . oh . . . ohhhhhh, nooooo, oh . . . Are those your fingerrrrrs . . . ?"

"They didn't touch me," said Guy. "I mean, they're really terrific, they don't try to be my friends or anything, they're just all chilly and wonderful. Last year, when I turned twenty-one, they gave me a card with this boy in a varsity sweater bowling on it; it said 'Happy Birthday Sixteen-Year-Old,' and they signed it 'Warm Regards, Your Parents,' I mean, I'd kill for them. But tonight they were just so odd, like aliens had replaced them with pods or something, although I guess it would be hard to tell, unless the pods hugged you, or wore blends or something. It's not their fault, really, maybe they're just getting old, and have mineral deficiencies. Boy, I hope they're okay."

"Moms and Dads," said someone, "who do they think they are?"

"Anyway," Guy continued, "my Dad puts down his paper, and my Mom starts crying, it was just really primitive, like those TV commercials where the black people cry because their children call them long distance. And then they said, 'Guy, if you need money, why don't you . . . why don't you . . . why . . . don't . . . you . . .' "

"Sell drugs?" someone suggested.

"Ask your Grandfather?" said another.

"Look in the desk?" said a third.

"It's all right, darling," said Venice, massaging Guy's shoulders. "How many syllables?"

"They said," said Guy, taking a deep breath, "they said, 'Why don't you, why don't you just . . . get . . . a . . . thing.' "

"Monstres!" gasped Caronia.

"Mais non!" echoed the crowd.

"This is a movie," whispered an agent, to his paid companion.

"A what, darling?" asked Venice, holding Guy's face in her hands. "What did they say you should get? A wallet?"

"A . . . j-j-j- . . . a job. A job."

There was a pause, as follows the discovery of a dismembered infant in a gully. Then the crowd began to jabber madly, turbulent with wrath and disbelief, supporting themselves on the urinals and wall dispensers (which offered combs, racy calling cards and pairs of magnetized scottie dogs).

"But that's insane!"

"Oh please, it must be a joke!"

"Who did you say these people were?"

"AIEEEEEEEEEEEEEEEEEEEEEE," moaned Licky, his orgasm capping the ferment. "Ohhhhh . . . oh, oh, OH . . . darling, very *nice!*"

"A job?" asked Venice, more puzzled than concerned. "Darling, you misunderstood. I mean, really."

"Gee, I don't think so," said Guy, slumping into the sink.

"Ju poor tink," said Ratallia, moving to Guy's side. "Ju shouldt rite pome. For ankuish."

As Ratallia touched Guy's arm, Venice felt a stab. She suspected appendicitis and clutched her side. She found only leather. What is this? Venice wondered. Then Ratallia looked deep into Guy's eyes.

Venice all but fell to the floor, as a slash of some unearthly fire ripped her consciousness. This was no physical pain, no mere rupture—this was jealousy. Ferocious, untrammeled, rampaging jealousy, a bloodthirsty panther unleashed at the picnic. Venice was astounded. She reeled; her gaze hardened to bulletproof plate, her spine grew rigid, sparking sabers burst from her fingertips. In a second's passage, Venice became a Saxon war machine, an unstoppable, unthinking murderess, a force able to raze villages, orphan children and leave other women to die, pinned beneath a stiletto heel.

Venice had never been in love before, so this was new. Venice found her entire being riveted to a scant inch of Guy's body, to the exact square of his arm currently occupied by Ratallia's index finger. Venice had always been an extreme person, but now her mind swarmed with thoughts of unparalleled savagery. Just who did that two-bit, no-talent Austrian geek think she was, anyway? Didn't Ratallia know how rapidly she could be shipped back to Vienna, in nineteen drenched parcels? Didn't Ratallia realize that there'd be trouble finding roles for an actress without a face?

Venice spoke with an even, chilling sound, a knell, each vowel ticking off a final ounce of Ratallia's life. *"No pomes,"* said Venice, hurling Ratallia into a bidet.

"Boy," said Guy, impressed.

"Who's next?" asked Venice, glaring around the lounge.

There were no takers, so Venice returned to Guy.

"What were you saying?" Venice asked.

"A job," said Guy, his misery returning. "I have to get one."

"Darling," said Licky, emerging from his stall, fulfilled and radiant. "A job? What is all this? Do I know you?"

"Guys," said Guy, to the assemblage, "I'm sorry, I'm fine, I don't want to make a fuss, go have a good time, it'll be fine. Thank you." Guy said all this in an utterly genuine tone, but there was a catch in his voice, so no one was fooled.

"Darling, I'm sorry," said someone.

"It's . . . unbelievable."

"I don't know what to say."

The crowd, hushed with compassion, moved gracefully from the room, stroking Guy's hand as they passed or touching his cheek. Everyone gave Venice a wide berth, as her gloved fists were still clenched. Once past the lounge area, everyone raced to the pay phones.

Gossip is the plasma of Manhattan; fresh gallons are pumped every second to keep the city alive. Everyone has to know everything, to feel involved, on top of it, securely soldered in the chain of intimate information. Anything can be taken as gossip, as fodder for rumor, innuendo and scandale. Even on slow days the wires blister.

"My dear, have you heard? Canned peaches are down to thirty-nine cents—could you *die?*"

"Darling, have you *seen* the new sanitation trucks—they're Bauhaus. *What* were they thinking of?"

"I've got to tell you—swear you won't repeat a *word;* this is *too* juicy—it's *Spring.*"

"Puss," said Venice, draping her arms around the little soldier.

"Don't worry," said Guy, kissing her hand.

"Darling, I'd love to have you as *my* maid," said Licky, "but, *quel dommage,* the position has been filled."

And then a freckled blond gymnast, recently defected from a state university, bounced out of Licky's stall and began to practice deep pliés near the hand blower.

"Isn't he heaven?" whispered Licky. "He'd give up his *life* for me. He thinks I run the City Ballet, can you imagine? *Where* does he get these ideas?"

"Darling," said Venice, "you'll find something. I know you will. Bite my tongue."

"Guy," said Caronia, "you will come to *Glaze!* Huggable!"

"Gee, *Glaze?*" repeated Guy, wonderingly. "Would I have to come in, like, every day?"

"Oh, no," said Caronia. "Say, two afternoons. For *texture.*"

"Would I have to wear, you know, a tie?" asked Guy.

"Never," said Caronia. "We encourage *innovation,* particularly in accessories. A stole!"

"Would I have to sit up?" asked Guy.

At this point both Guy and Caronia realized the kindness, and the futility, of Caronia's offer, and the discussion ended. Unfortunately, the building the magazine's offices occupied had stairs.

"Guys, I'm fine, really," said Guy, embarrassed at the distress he was causing those closest to him. "Let's go dance." He paused, and then asked, solely for information, "Uhm, does anybody have a noose?"

"So brave," Caronia murmured to Venice, as the group scoured their evening bags for nooses and, finding only cream shadow, did their eyes instead.

"Jai am sad for ju," said Ratallia, climbing out of the bidet, "but ju mek Ratallia vet."

"It's all positively Jacobean," said Licky. "Madness, vengeance, mutilating poverty, desperate dynasties swimming in spirochetes, the innocent brought low—do you have my check?"

Guy handed him his mother's stipend, and Licky kissed him on both cheeks, as if for the last time. "Darling, whatever you decide," Licky said, "remember—I'd like the Coca-Cola thing from the loft, and the dog." Licky tossed a fluid length of beige chiffon over his shoulder and exited. The gymnast repeated the kiss, weeping.

"God help you," the gymnast said, and he leapt out after Licky.

"Boy, I'm such a dope," said Guy, looking in the mirror and, for additional drama, squeezing the button on the liquid soap funnel.

"Darling," said Venice, soothingly, "I'd like a divorce."

"What?" said Guy, horrified.

"Just kidding," said Venice, nibbling his ear.

6

Personnel

Everyone flowed toward the dance floor, but Guy needed to be alone. He trudged up the stairs to the catwalk, the iron arc on which he had spotted Venice the night before. Guy moved soberly to the center of the bridge, with a measured tread, almost a march. He envisioned himself walking a plank, although the overall effect was more that of someone measuring a room for wall-to-wall carpeting. Guy made a smart parade pivot and faced the hall. He decided he should have a blindfold, for anyone to really get it. His shoulders began to ache, so he sat down, his heels dangling in the air over the dancers' heads. He acknowledged a friend's concerned face or a "thumbs up" signal with a chipper little wave, but that was all.

Money, Guy thought. When you have it you never think about it, but when it's gone there's nothing else on your mind.

As Guy turned to lie on his stomach, it began to rain. It was just a light drizzle, but it was one of the Club's few annoying effects, created with a sprinkler system and a callous disregard for anyone in silk georgette. The coatcheck girls shook aluminum sheets, sounding a muffled thunder, and flashes of strobe bolted from the balcony. Flat, painted canvas clouds, strung on wires, were tugged slowly across the theater's screen. The clouds had blustery little faces, and scrawny cartoon arms hoisting umbrellas. Soon the Club grew sodden and fogbound, as if a wet blanket had actually been tossed over the premises.

For only the fourth time in his life, Guy contemplated suicide. The other occasions had been nothing—bad haircuts, a chocolate bar that had gone all stale and powdery, losing a phone number, the common sources of self-mutilation. Until tonight, the pain issue had always halted Guy's attempts to kill himself. All the really picturesque forms of death sounded stupendously painful, and Guy was the sort of person the dentist had to knock out completely, even for X rays. Guy didn't like pain, it didn't agree with him, and this embarrassed him; people were always saying that pain was the next thing, right after reggae. Guns and knives—Guy had heard that even pills hurt because you die with a stomach ache.

But what if I fell to my death, Guy thought, envisioning his ragdoll form as it twisted through the downpour. No, he decided, I might land on someone, one of the dancers, and injure them, or at least ruin their evening. Guy comforted himself by picturing his own funeral. Everyone would be sad, and they would say wonderful things about him and sob over what a loss it was. Guy felt transported to the ceremony itself; he found himself standing amid the mourners. He started to sniffle, moved by the devotion of his friends and family. Venice was starkly resplendent in black lace toreadors; I married the most beautiful widow on Earth, Guy thought, his eyes moist. And look, there was Licky with the dog. Ratallia Parv was weeping over the open coffin, especially after Venice slammed the lid on her fingers, and there was Lucy Membrane as a pallbearer, hefting the casket on a sturdy shoulder. Caronia declaimed at graveside, delivering a wrenching eulogy. Guy couldn't quite make out what Caronia was saying; all he could catch was "Death! Hatable!" and "Black! Ebony! Onyx! Ah, *cortège!*"

And there, by the bier itself, as the coffin was lowered to the grave, there were Guy's parents. Guy wept openly now, at the vision of their inconsolable, wracked faces. Guy's father put his arm around Guy's mother. Mrs. Huber searched the heavens, moaning, "If only we hadn't . . . "

"Guy!" Licky screamed, as he scrambled up the stair to the catwalk. "Good news! It's too fabulous!"

"I know," said Guy, still in mid-funeral, raising his face into a cloudburst. "Boy, what a beautiful ceremony."

"The door, the new one," Licky said, breathlessly kneeling beside his friend. "He's dead!"

"What?" asked Guy, shaken from his hallucination. "The door? He's dead? You mean, as far as you're concerned?"

"No," said Licky scornfully, "not that bad. He's been killed!"

"What?" said Guy.

"These total icks, from Minneapolis, they shot him. They were purest A&P safari look. They were sublime, but they had real live guns, can you imagine? They couldn't get in, and then the woman yelled, 'This doesn't happen at Knotts Berry Farm!' and then blammo! Isn't it wild? I mean, with those outfits, you'd think they'd just carry garden hoses, or pole lamps, don't you think?"

"Gee," said Guy, "I guess so."

"Darling!" called Venice from below, covering her head with a back issue of *Glaze*, "it's too perfect!"

"What is?" asked Guy.

"Darling," said Licky, rolling his eyes at Guy's dimness, "you can be the new door! It's a job!"

"The new door?" said Guy. "You think?"

"Do it," commanded Venice, as the rain began to abate and the fog to roll out.

"Come on," said Licky, dragging Guy toward the stair. As they clambered down, the painted rainclouds jerked and moved off the screen. The sprinklers shut down and the warmer lights, the amber gels, began to beam. A story-high yellow sunburst fell from the rafters onto the screen. The sunburst had a toothy smile and batted thick cellophane lashes (the lashes were operated manually by two union stagehands). The dancers looked up as hundreds of beach thongs were fired from cylinders on the walls.

"You'll love it," said Licky, as they reached the dance floor. "We'll go see the crooks!"

"The crooks?" Guy asked, confused but brightening.

"Darling," said Venice, "the owners!"

Licky led Guy and Venice to the rear of the dance floor and took them behind the movie screen (everyone was far too excited to even begin considering the metaphor). There was a narrow passage, and Licky located a nondescript iron door; beyond this lay a rotting stairway. Licky pushed the Hubers along.

"Does the Mafia really own the Club?" asked Guy.

"Of course," said Licky. "The Mafia owns everything, at least everything that makes a profit. Mobsters are heaven, lots of gold chains and sleazoid open shirts and lounge-act chest hair, you'll go mad. They just scoop the money into plastic garbage bags and take it to their mothers in Queens. It's really very touching, except when they hang people from meathooks and break kneecaps and things."

"Wait, will they break my kneecaps?" Guy hesitated.

"Darling, of course not," said Licky. "They'll adore you, now hurry up, we'll just ask for personnel."

The stairway twisted and turned, infiltrating the jumble of tubing, meters and generators that lit, irrigated and air-conditioned the Club de. Bits of the premises' past lives surfaced along the way: a torn, yellowing showcard from a De Mille epic; a chorine's plume caught in a railing; an autographed photo of some forgotten celebrity panelist. Finally a wooden door with peeling paint appeared.

"Here goes," said Licky.

Venice flipped her hair and adjusted her cleavage, briskly. "I'm ready," she said. "Are they?"

"This is so exciting!" said Guy, dying to meet real criminals.

Licky knocked, and a distinctly urban, female voice beckoned, "Hoi! Comeawn in!"

The trio entered a cinderblock storeroom. The walls were lined with cardboard cartons of soft drinks and tonic waters stacked almost to the ceiling. There was also a card table, a Sony 19″ portable television and a swiveling wooden desk chair on casters, with a cushion on the seat. A throne had been constructed from a group of the cartons, and a woman had slung herself across it. The woman wore a minuscule crocheted bikini and high-heeled lamé sandals. She had a deep, orangy tan, and her fingernails and toenails were painted with tiny stripes. Her hair was blinding platinum, teased sky-high, and suspiciously immobile. Guy had never met such a woman. Could she be a mermaid, he wondered, unable to live above basement level?

"Hoi," the woman repeated, dangling a sandal from one toe. "Howya' doin'?"

"We're too swell," said Licky. "Darling, first, you look fabulous, I can't tell you. And second, are the owners around?"

"Nah. They hadda go somewheres. They're gettin' Chinese or somethin'. I'm Jakkie. With two K's, see?" The woman pointed to an elaborate charm she wore about her neck, which spelled out her name in diamond chips. "I'm in charge, ya know, for now."

"Ah," said Licky, "then you are just the lady we want to see. Jakkie, *mon image*, the new door's been shot!"

"He wuz shot? Jeez, but the owners ain't even here, I wonda who shotum?"

"Oh, just someone, darling—you know, an assassin. The important thing is, you're going to need someone new, and I have just the ticket, the answer, Mister Everything. Jakkie," Licky announced, "this is Guy."

"Hoi, Goi," said Jakkie, giggling at the strange wit of the greeting.

"Hi, Jakkie," said Guy, holding out his hand. "How are you?"

"Foin," said Jakkie, refusing Guy's hand, as her nails were wet.

"This is Venice," said Guy, proudly, "my wife."

"Darling," said Venice, mesmerized by Jakkie's hair.

"Hoi," said Jakkie. "Whatcha lookin' at?"

"Oh," said Venice, "your hair. It's special. Where do you buy it?"

"Uhm," said Jakkie, "I goddit at, uhm . . . the Wig-Wam, on Fourteenth Street, it's really, like, durable. It's callt 'Polar Rhapsody,' an' ya can also geddit in, uhm, pink, wit' little braidy things."

"Really," said Venice, amazed.

"Now, Jakkie," Licky interrupted, eager to settle matters. "You've got to help us. It's an American tragedy. Guy has been tossed out by his family, they have turned their backs, they have driven him from their very bosom, and we just hate their filthy guts, *n'est-ce pas?*"

"We do?" asked Guy, taken aback.

"We do," said Venice, encouraging Licky's flow.

"Guy has no skills," Licky continued, "no previous experience, just a loft, a trust fund and an Ivy League diploma. He's utterly useless."

"It's embarrassing," Venice confided.

"It is," Guy confirmed.

"Now, Guy won't take handouts," Licky warned.

"Yes I will!" Guy all but shouted.

"He's very proud," Licky declared, glaring at Guy. "He just wants a chance to work, to lend a hand, to be of some human value on this Godforsaken planet."

Licky grabbed Guy's chin, holding Guy's face up to the light.

"Owww," said Guy, as Licky had grabbed awfully hard.

"Just look at him," Licky demanded. "Look at this well-fed, well-bred, shiny little face, this airborne little basket case, this throw pillow with feet. Can we turn him away? Can we say, 'Darling, I'm sorry, the position has been filled'? Can we say, 'No, you have nothing to contribute, nothing besides a few dance steps and fabulous hair'? Can we do that, Jakkie? Can we toss this wretched little Teddy bear back in the toy box, and nail the lid?"

"I love it," said Venice.

"It's so sad," said Guy, his eyes misting.

Jakkie was an easy mark for a sob story. Every month she pilfered a few dollars from a protection racket and sent the money to a Nicaraguan orphan with big eyes. Licky suspected this and pulled Guy's eyelids open all the way. Guy cocked his head wistfully.

"Don't push it," said Venice.

"Gee . . . " said Jakkie. Just yesterday she had donated some of her old babydoll nighties to the Battered Women's Shelter. People always said, Jakkie, you're too nice for your own good.

"Okey-doke," said Jakkie. I got no choice, she thought, that poor kid. And his wife is kinda cute, even if she don't know how to do her face.

"Ya can be the new door," Jakkie told Guy. "It's awright by me."

"Thanks!" said Guy. "Jakkie, you're so terrific!"

"Darling," said Venice. *"Quel* saint."

"Please, have a Fresca," Licky insisted, unleashing a can from its plastic web. "We insist."

"Thanks," said Jakkie, utterly charmed, rolling the cool can across her forehead.

"Gee, this is so great," said Guy. "When should I start? You know, being the door?"

"Uhm . . . tomorrow night," Jakkie decided. "Jus' don' let in nobody who ain't right. Got it?"

"I'll do my best," said Guy, solemnly, putting his hand over his heart.

"Yeah, ya gotta be careful," said Jakkie. "It's pretty nutsy up there."

"It's a sacred trust," said Licky, "a priesthood, a coronet and more. And now we really must go. Jakkie, you are a shrine, a savior and one hellish little mantrap. Tell the owner we are at your bejeweled feet, and he must give you more responsibility, your own casino at the very least. Your own call-girl ring. Your own Senator!"

"I'll tellum!" said Jakkie, inspired. "I been workin' real hard!"

"I kiss you forever!" said Licky, heading out the door.

"We'll talk," promised Venice.

"Bye!" said Guy. "And thanks again!"

"Mmmmm," said Venice, kissing Guy once they were in the hallway. "My breadwinner!"

"Your parents will be so proud," said Licky. "They'll just burst!"

"It's such a good idea," said Guy, marveling, "I won't have to get up early!"

Guy's depression had now totally dispersed. He felt ashamed of himself for having moped so. Guy's natural high spirits, his eagerness to enjoy life, returned in full.

By this time, word of Guy's status as the new door had spread throughout the Club, and a distant huzzah went up.

"Fabulous," said Venice, listening to the cheers.

"Oh, you guys," said Guy, grinning, his face ablaze with Venice's lipstick. "It's just a job!"

7

Hair

Everyone awoke the next day pleased as could be, just knowing Guy would be on the door that evening. The teletypes churned, and people forgot all about the hostage situation in Sri Lanka. Jakkie told the Club's owners she had hired Guy, and they were more than satisfied. The owners even bought Jakkie a kitten as a bonus. Jakkie was thrilled, and she named the kitty Jakkie II. Ratallia Parv ice-packed a bruise on her thigh. Dot Wenice, Ratallia thought, che vus so mean to Ratallia. Vot did Ratallia do to her? Vot a vurld.

Caronia Desti commanded a sidebar in her magazine listing Guy and Venice among the city's Ten Most Visible Couples (Contessa Larini had remarried in order to make the list). The sun shone, the planet watusied, all nature was in jubilee. Licky, Venice and Guy longed to share their feelings with one another, but they all woke up many blocks, if not boroughs, apart.

. . .

Venice opened her left eye around one o'clock as the bed swayed gently beneath her. Confused, she opened her right eye as well, in a spirit of real investigation.

"Guy?" she murmured, wondering why the loft had suddenly developed a porthole. Was it Licky's idea?

Fully awake, Venice looked around. She saw lavish French furniture, and family oil portraits, and more portholes. I'm on a yacht, she realized, but whose yacht? How did I get here? Think, she thought to herself, where have I been? She and Guy had spent a heady evening celebrating Guy's new job. They'd done the town, up, down, mid and cross, they'd frequented the sides, East and West, the Villages, West and East, Tribeca, SoHo, NoHo, even that perverse little patch of riverbank Licky had dubbed Teehee, but where had it all led? How had the newlyweds been separated? Were they legally separated? Sometimes, all it took to finish a marriage was a dispute over who was tired, and who wanted to try that new place. But Venice couldn't recall any argument, only a relay of cabs and cars and maybe a carriage of some sort, and a stop for gelato, and finishing a bottle so it wouldn't go to waste.

I really should leave breadcrumbs, Venice decided, so I can find my life.

Tugging the sheet around her, Venice sat up in bed. She looked around the stateroom, but she seemed to be alone.

"Darling?" she called out, always a good opener. Venice couldn't remember when she had started using "darling"; it might have been her first word, uttered at a tub toy or pediatrician. Venice liked to be on intimate terms with the world. She would plot herself bargaining with the Soviets, opening the session with "Yuri, darling." "Darling" disarms people. They suspect you know their secrets and approve. Venice had only doubted her sanity when she had caught herself calling a tree "darling"; she hadn't been watching her step and had walked smack into a local oak. *"Darling,"* she'd told the tree.

There was a knock on the stateroom door.

"Darling?" Venice said.

The door opened and a uniformed ensign stepped into the room.

"Darling," Venice said.

"Good afternoon, ma'am," the ensign said. "Mr. Carlingcurl has asked that I tender his apologies, as he has been unavoidably called away."

"Mr. Carlingcurl?" Venice repeated. The name was completely unfamiliar.

"This is Mr. Carlingcurl's yacht," the ensign said. "He has flown to the Montana factories. He has asked that I give you this, as a token of his affection."

The ensign presented Venice with a leather box, with filigree tooling. Venice opened the box. Inside was a pair of diamond earrings, perfect solitaires.

"Look," said Venice, admiring the earrings. "Breakfast."

"They're very beautiful, ma'am," the ensign commented.

"You think?" asked Venice, holding an earring up to the light. She thought for a moment and then put the earring on.

"Cab fare," she informed the ensign. "Guaranteed by the Constitution."

Thinking a moment longer, Venice realized how nice the remaining earring would look in Guy's ear.

"For my husband," Venice told the ensign, slipping the other earring into her bag.

"Very good, ma'am," the ensign said. "Mr. Carlingcurl has placed the ship at your disposal. Would you care to go ashore?"

"I suppose," said Venice, stretching voluptuously. She looked around the stateroom.

"Men," she said, shaking her head. "What can you do?"

"Tell me about it," said the ensign, taking his leave.

. . .

Soon Venice was aboard a launch, headed for the mainland. The ensign piloted the craft. Venice sat in the rear of the launch, her face to the wind.

"I don't think I slept with Mr. Carlingcurl, do you, darling?" Venice asked the ensign. "I'm a married woman."

"I wouldn't know, ma'am."

"I think I was at a party on the yacht, and I fell asleep under the coats on the bed."

"Very good, ma'am."

"No," said Venice, thinking harder. "There were no cabs—that's it. Of course. There were no cabs, so I just hailed a passing yacht."

"I like that one," said the ensign, navigating a swell.

"That's not sex," Venice concluded, "that's just . . . just . . . "

"Transportation," the ensign suggested.

"Darling," said Venice.

"Where shall I put in?" asked the ensign, as the launch neared shore.

"Where?" said Venice. "Well, let me see. I've got to do something for my husband; tonight is such a big step. What do wives do when their husbands go off to work?"

"Bake a pie?" the ensign offered.

"Buy a pie?" Venice countered.

"Steal a pie?" the ensign parried.

"No," said Venice, "that's not it. I know. My hair. That's what I'll do for Guy—my *hair.*"

The cab left Venice deep within the roiling henna'd vortex of the Hair District. There are blocks of Manhattan allotted to flowers, and the garment industry, but the Hair District, a concentration of stylists, colorists and laboratories, roars out of control. Hair is central to city life. Hair is the barometer of the soul. Every head puts forth a certain quantity of hair, and it demands tending, fuss, decision. Man is the only animal who owns a comb.

Venice headed for Greer Schlesinger's building, as a person of greater awareness. Greer was the very freshest tressmaster, a sweet, illiterate young man who seemed to exist without a first language. Hair was all Greer knew and all he cared to know. Greer found in blunt cuts and highlighting what others have known in the sonata and the fresco. More than a technician; more, really, than an artist—Greer was a saint of hair.

Greer's Hair Studio occupied a half-floor in a born-again brownstone. The Studio was announced by a screamingly discreet brass plaque set in the front door, which read "Greer Schlesinger, I.D.L., O.O.B." This denoted Greer's election to the International Do League, and his recent award, in Geneva, of the coveted Order of the Bang (he wore his Ringlet Cluster on only the most formal occasions).

Venice entered the Studio and, as always, felt as if she were penetrating someone's trance. The Studio was designed for isolation and calm, in tones of lavender and greige. There were no corners and no direct sources of light. There was music, a dull electronic bleat, the sound of an EKG, a monitor for heart patients. Patrons were asked to remove their shoes. Venice retired to a changing cubicle to don a lavender smock. There was something infinitely serious about the Studio, something devout and hushed and unsaid. Venice understood this atmosphere and respected it.

A minion rinsed Venice's hair, in a low basin, and then Venice was brought to a high plexiglass stool, where Greer would attend her. Venice was completely relaxed; she turned her head in wide circles, releasing her neck. She gazed in the circle of mirror on the wall before her, her hair hanging in damp strands, as wet clay, tempting the sculptor.

"*Hi,*" breathed Greer, appearing from the mist. Greer was

a boneless, milky fellow, virginal in his mohair jumpsuit. At times Venice suspected that Greer was truly not all there, that major portions of his anatomy were holograms, projections of edge and shadow.

"Darling," said Venice, "I can't wait."

"Mmmmm . . . " said Greer, already beyond Venice, awaiting astral instruction as he twisted his pearls. Greer never left the Studio. He subsisted on microbiotics, acupuncture for his tormented wrists, and hibernation on a thin cotton pallet. A grateful client had embroidered the pallet with a hairdresser's creed as a birthday token. The pallet read, "I Just Want to Curl Up and Dye."

Venice did not speak during her cut; chatter would seem flippant, playing tag with one's surgeon during a quadruple bypass. Like all great urban beauties, Venice understood maintenance, the day labor of remaining gasp-worthy. Venice refused to allow her face to usurp all daily concerns, but she was no fool.

Venice's makeup kit was not the flowered satin zip-up of the dilettante but the steel tackle box of the professional. Venice mixed and blended, shading with Tintoretto delicacy. She maintained a full palette, of tawny sand and cerulean dawn and sienna remorse. She collected sponges and wands and puffs. She stocked clay masque and fetal collagen scrub and oil of aloe. She hoarded ultra-lashes and twelve-hour toner and T-zone controlling mousse. Venice's full cargo weighed over twenty pounds, and yet she never appeared made-up.

When a pimple would bud, Venice would enter a requiem state and consider the moral implications of the blemish. Was she being convicted of something? Had a sin gone unscourged? Could anyone love a person with a pimple, or would romance become a mercy situation?

Hair, though, is the ultimate trial. A bad haircut can disfigure a person for weeks, forcing her to sit home, praying that everyone will assume she has hepatitis rather than a cowlick. Hair shock, Venice knew, the forty-eight-hour period following even a minor trim, accounts for fifty percent of all bad hats. A person with a new haircut is naked, disoriented, altogether alone—am I Garbo or Harpo? Venus or Pluto? creation . . . or victim?

"Remember that girl, one of Tanzo's," Licky often cautioned. "Greer did her, she left, and they found her downtown three days later, just wandering, with one sock. For two weeks all she could say was, 'But I don't want a shag.' Now she lives with her parents."

Venice had shut her eyes for most of her cut, concentrating on thoughts of Guy and other pleasant distractions. Now she noted Greer's contented whimper as the lulling keen of the blow-dryer ceased. Venice opened her eyes, and other clients began to hover, in every phase of treatment, from jellied pincurls to tin-foil streaking cap to lustrefix hot oil bombardment. Harpies, fates, vultures—every look was accounted for.

"*Look* at *that.*"

"Well, it's new, isn't it?"

"It's an attempt."

"Disturbing."

"I see DiRicardi's influence, but there's an immediacy, a, what would you call it, a whole new *feeling* for length."

"I . . . I . . . I'm sorry, does anyone have a tissue, Greer, it's . . . *beyond* . . . it's . . . Greer, I haven't been able to weep since my son died. Thank you, thank you . . . "

"Ahead of its time."

"Interesting."

"My four-year-old could do that."

"It will change the way we see hair; from today, no one will *dare* back-comb again."

"No solution."

"Stature, but not without humor."

"Freedom must never be confused with license."

"Obscene . . . spitting in the street . . . "

"The 'Belle Epoque' . . . the pageboy . . . the beehive . . . *Schlesinger.*"

"I want the *exact* same thing, only two inches longer in the back. I have a *chicken* neck, I *hate* my neck, I could *kill* my neck."

"A masterwork."

"A lie."

"The future."

"It's fabulous," Venice pronounced, thoroughly satisfied. "It's the best. It's *sex.*"

Venice retrieved her fur and left the Studio. She tossed her head and jumped up and down, shaking off the afternoon's attention. Venice liked taking care of herself, but a session at Greer's could all but suffocate. Enough beauty, Venice thought; I want a candy bar.

"Hair shock," Venice told a passing policeman. "Where is the funding?"

8

Message Units

As Venice left the Hair District, Licky stirred atop a waterbed in a different state. The waterbed sloshed and rolled and Licky felt vaguely queasy. The bed filled much of a tarnished airstream trailer, an aluminum mobile home hitched to a used car. Both vehicles were parked in a lot on the outskirts of Ho-Ho-Kus, New Jersey.

The trailer was creaky and musty and reeked of incense; sex has to be awfully good to excuse incense. Licky looked to either side, examining the remains of the night—the cigarette butts and the cheeseburger styrofoam and the snoring men.

After agenting Guy into a position at the Club de, Licky had decided to reward himself. Licky and his gymnast had left the Club at dawn in search of bawdier entertainment. Somewhere in their travels they had found a bodybuilder. Ultimately the ménage had retired to the bodybuilder's trailer.

Licky liked to think of himself as a romantic. He announced new loves, the laciest of valentines, on the hour. In truth he was less a passionflower than a gourmand, an appreciator of finesse and variation. Licky found muscles extraordinary, especially in a world where they had rare practical application. Licky's bulging favorites displayed a Lillian Russell allure, they tortured themselves into hefty hourglass abundance, into three-layer beefcake. Sex with these men was strenuous, a triathlon, a day in the fields. Afterward, Licky was always surprised to find that he had merely had intercourse, and not repaired a transmission or timbered a ranch house.

Licky felt no compulsion to develop his own physique; he remained a jockey, a buoy cresting a sea of brawn. The evening had been more than satisfactory, with the gymnast coaxed into untenable positions, the bodybuilder serving as a mattress, and Licky doing all the talking. This, Licky thought as he surveyed his snoozing companions, this is what God really did on the seventh day. Licky had enjoyed himself, but then Licky always did. Licky viewed men less as lovers than as rides.

Licky's true heart, which did exist, contrary to popular belief, lay elsewhere. He slipped into one of the bodybuilder's enormous, rank T-shirts and inhaled deeply. He grew centered, anointed, worthy of a deeper emotion. It's time, Licky thought, savoring the suspense, his palms moist. Nestling in the covers, Licky reached for his soulmate, his witch's familiar, the only one who really understood: the telephone.

Licky had experienced a difficult birth, he had been loath to leave the womb, well aware of how torturous it is to find a decent apartment. Only the Circean chime of a ringing phone had coaxed Licky from his mother. "It's for me!" the babe had cawed. Licky's love for the instrument was infinite, yielding, affectingly dependent. There was a need and a rapture to the affair, an iconic quality reminiscent of the golden Madonnas with Phone.

Yet there is also an eroticism here. Licky cherished the phone for its tactile joys: for the plastic's lubricious gleam, for the receiver's welcoming curve, for the seduction of lips and ear, for the dial tone's ravishing purr. Call-waiting, call-forwarding, conference calls—the connections were myriad. The phone knew what a guy wanted; just a touch and it throbbed. Licky was a slave to the phone, a willing drone. Snorting, he gripped the little Princess.

"You whore," Licky told the receiver, as he began to dial.

By midafternoon, Licky had spoken with the following numbers, charging all of the calls to Guy's credit card: his seven best friends (to dissect Guy's new job), six possible friends ("My Waiting List," Licky called them, reserving judgment until their test scores and fees were in), four hostesses (to R.S.V.P. for parties he had not been invited to), three multi-millionaires he'd met at the Club (never just millionaires, "Why bother," he'd say), fifty nobodies (to cancel lunch after standing them up), Guy's mother (to borrow a bag), his horoscope ("I'm old-fashioned," he'd say, "I love the moonlight"), his dealer (an eleven-year-old in Harlem who drove an exquisitely restored Bugatti; "My idea," Licky would say), his couturier (for late-breaking hemlines), five masseurs (arranging a birthday surprise for himself) and ten enemies in other time zones (just to wake them and hang up).

Licky had not spoken to his mother in over a year, as she was unable to get a call through. It all came down to plotting an evening: Licky craved every conceivable option. He wanted to know what everyone was doing, and he wanted to be asked, even if he couldn't possibly do it all. Licky froze people on hold, and had the operator disrupt the calls of others, Licky bribed and juggled and cross-referenced his way to the most fun imaginable.

Finally, Licky called his employer, to make sure that Guy had something decent to wear at the Club that night (Licky being the compleat gentleman's gentleman). Licky let the phone ring, but there was no one in at the loft. Licky tried to picture an activity he would not interrupt to answer the phone. He ran through sex, murder and death itself, but he could not turn up anything sufficiently competitive.

By now the receiver was smoking, fried from overuse. Licky let the liquid resin drip to the floor, tying up the Hubers' line indefinitely. Seizing a slab of the waking bodybuilder, Licky moaned, "Can you believe it? I love those Hubers, but really—how am I supposed to get any work done?"

9

Something to Wear

While Venice began the day at sea and Licky found himself in New Jersey, Guy awoke under the unlikeliest circumstances of all: alone in his own home. Women had pursued him, but Guy had resisted. Guy liked sex but not the surrounding effort. Infidelity would be so complicated; you'd have to talk to someone, at least a little; figure out where to go, get there; get undressed, have sex; get dressed, and find a cab. Just the thought of it would send Guy to bed for a week.

Guy brought laziness to a level of almost total empathy. He could glance at an advertisement for cornflakes, and his body would assume the toil of a fieldhand, wracked from the corn harvest and the shucking bee. This was why Guy never read the paper or watched the news on TV—he was terrified of absorbing the world's vitality, of incurring an international sleep debt and never leaving the sheets. Sex with Venice was transcendent exertion. Guy awoke at noon, wishing Venice was beside him. Guy began to imagine all the things he and his wife might do together. Just the thought winded him, and he was forced to nap.

Rising at one, Guy recalled his imminent employment. Tonight he would be a door at the Club de. Would it be hard? Would it be fun? Was there an ethical struggle involved? Would there be unconscionable stress? Would there be violence? Will I like it, Guy wondered, will I hate it, will I get sick, will I have a great time? Am I qualified to serve as a heedless umpire of Manhattan nightlife, as an infallible sentinel, as a social godhead? Am I worthy? And, most importantly, what should I wear?

A job, Guy pondered—gee, I've dressed for every occasion but this. Guy reasoned as any man might, confronting onrushing duty. Guy became a general girding for battle, a President facing reelection, an astronaut shuttling toward Saturn. I guess I have to do what a man's got to do, Guy resolved. I have to go shopping.

Guy moved to the loft's wall of windows. He placed his hands on the sill and beheld the city's shops. He felt as early man must have, standing erect and facing the dawning sky. There was a sense of limitless possibility, of frontier, of a field of pristine, just-fallen snow, aching for imprint. There was a spiritual rush—all those *things* out there, eager to be fondled and considered and adopted. Guy was magnetized, infused, his fingers itched. The urge to splurge took hold.

Guy liked to shop for almost anything, but clothing was the supreme shiver. Clothing was the most intimate of purchases, the procurement of a skin, a personality, a statement. Shopping for clothes renders psychoanalysis unnecessary, every schizophrenic leaning can be explored and sated. Guy collected clothes; he shopped as if possessed, as if seeking a fix, or a natural parent. Guy elevated materialism from a doctrine to a fever. Guy knew that if he looked good, he would feel terrific, whole, shielded. Why would anyone need a therapist when there were so many Italian designers?

Guy downed a carton of orange juice, for the day would demand persistence and stamina. People who knew Guy would have been astonished, as his midday drowse was replaced with a superhuman vigor, and his bedroom eyes went wide. Guy became a hunter, fated to stalk the retail wilds, his adrenaline pumping, his every sense dedicated to cornering the elusive prey. Yes, Guy would shop, and he would win; he would refuse to return without an ensemble lashed to the fender of his taxi, without a shirt or sock suitable for mounting beside previous kills.

Guy began by canvassing the city's department stores, those stolid democracies of style, those jolly gargantuas trumpeting white sales, housewares and notions, those brimming, marked-down monoliths where one might bring the family and spend the dollar days. There is too much to look at in these stores, and nothing to buy except quilted shoe caddies which hang on the backs of closet doors, and clean underwear. Guy made lightning tours of these clip'n'save, Misses Better wastelands, barely stopping to touch or price. Guy was such an experienced shopper that he could close his eyes and trail his fingertips over a rack of garments, sensing fiber content and stitches per inch with the accuracy of the blind, or the Bond Street ancient.

Guy knew he wouldn't find anything at the department stores, but he visited out of habit and gratitude. These had been his first stores, where he had cut his teeth. Children love department stores, because at Christmas Santa sits in the toy department. Santa, Guy had always believed, was the inventor of shopping. Actually, Guy was never sure if he had believed in Santa or just in R. H. Macy and Lord & Taylor. They all seemed equally benevolent men. Guy couldn't omit the department stores from his spree—he owed them.

His debt discharged, Guy struck out for the reefs of smaller boutiques which lined the upper avenues. These shops exist to intimidate. They are places where shoppers buy things just to prove they can. Guy was intrigued by the sales help at these shops. They were the only people in Manhattan who did less than he did. These sales help are a hothouse species, consumed with exactly how far to push up their sleeves. They do not ignore customers—they do not *see* customers. They recognize only one another, thanks to the cologne. Manhattan waiters are arrogant, but they do eventually arrive, nibbling your French fries. Sales-clerks refuse to serve at any time. They will deny garments to the wrong people. "This top wouldn't be happy with someone like you," they sniff. They don't sell things, they place them.

The goods overseen by these huffy covens are rarely desirable. Guy poked around, scrutinizing Tanzo Matta's spring line for "Men," as Tanzo called them. The pieces all had one armhole too many, or a strange pocket hanging off a knee, for alms, or required hairstyles Guy was not ready to consider. These shops answer the question, "Where did he *find* something like that?"

The traditional men's stores proved equally barren. Guy valued gabardine and worsted, but the corporate tailoring made him feel stony, encased, like a male impersonator. The sporting goods centers also disappointed, aswim with crushed velour jogging suits and endorsed wristbands. Guy left quickly, although he did approve of clothing that indicated but did not require physical activity.

The search grew long, but Guy refused to panic. To the power shopper, the chase rejuvenates. Shoppers rule Manhattan, they cover the most ground. Guy felt he was gobbling the city up, seeking a nugget, a jewel, the prize hidden deep within the popcorn and caramel.

Finally Guy headed toward the most expensive and exclusive markets of all, the shoppers' mecca. Guy's taxi approached the

Bowery, home of derelicts and mission work, a war zone of crumbling tenements and Ukrainian luncheonettes. Reaching an especially seedy block, Guy directed the driver toward a flock of limousines idling by the curb.

Guy left the cab and strode toward a seemingly gutted building, the windows sealed with cinderblocks. There was no door, just a black maw. Above the gap was cardboard reading "The Deering-Rant Thyroid Thrift Outlet, God Bless The Cheerful Donation."

Deering-Rant is one of the city's leading thrift shops. It is administered by an uptown hospital, The Deering-Rant Thyroid and Related Disorders Medical Facility. The shop is staffed with elderly volunteers—stooped, skeptical women in print dresses, fierce gnomes Doing Good.

Guy stepped into the store. A flinty woman in blue rinse and crocheted bolero was chatting on the phone with a customer. She turned to a co-worker, her hand over the receiver.

"Sheik Oded Ben Fadood would like forty bowling shirts, fifty mouton chubbies and anything we've got in a letter sweater," the woman said. "Write it down, Vera; you know how you forget."

Guy glowed. Deering-Rant was just about his favorite store. He contemplated a battered toaster that was missing its cord.

"I'm sorry, dear, that's been sold," said a crone in hair net and aluminum walker. "Contessa Larini has a hold on it."

"That's okay," said Guy, "I'm looking for something to wear."

"Join the club, dear," said the crone, who found volunteering at Deering-Rant far more satisfying than either the bookmobile or chowing those brats on the hot lunch program.

"I need something really great," Guy confided. He decided to play his ace. "For my job."

Guy knew his way around an older woman.

"Well, isn't that nice," said the crone, so pleased. "What a fine young man. Come, dear, let's have a look. We've just received a lovely big shipment, from the nicest woman; she said please not to tell her husband that she's giving his things away, but they're falling apart and he looks like a hobo. Why, here they are, from Nine Twenty Park, these great big boxes, we'll just snip the string. You might also look in the basement, we have some ironing pads and a few single shoes, although we usually put those aside for Mr. Banes. Now whatever you do, don't ask that new girl for help—look at her, the *wattles*. She steals, I just know it; she's ravaged the cardigans."

"Gee, these look wonderful," said Guy, stacking the boxes. He trembled with anticipation. Such a hoard demanded privacy.

"Thank you so much," Guy told the crone. "And excuse me, but, did your eye fall out?"

"Not again," sighed the crone. "Oh dear, has it rolled off?"

"I think so," Guy improvised. "I think it went under the table with all the rainhats."

"Thank you, dear, you're a godsend," said the crone, tottering off.

"Good luck, ma'am!" Guy called out. He felt guilty, but he was alone with the boxes. He hustled his booty to a far corner, cackling, the first white man to set eyes on Angkor Wat.

Other customers soon noticed Guy's activities in the corner.

"What's he doing?" asked one customer. "It's not oven mitts, is it?"

"What's he got?" demanded another. "Is that chiffon, buddy?"

"Get him!" howled a third, certain she smelled rotting ankle-strap wedgies.

Guy was almost ripped to pieces as the crowd jumped on him. The cartons flew into the air, raining faded plaid boxer shorts, moth-eaten tennis sweaters and an incomplete deck of playing cards.

"Take 'em!" Guy yelled, hurling some old army blankets into the fray. Clutching something black, he bounded across the plywood tables, fending off shoppers with the heel of his motorcycle boot and the back of his hand. Eventually Guy reached the register, where another volunteer awaited, once a Ziegfeld glory, then a Fifth Avenue matron, and now an active widow.

"Hello, dear," said the woman. "What have we here?"

"It's so neat," said Guy, sharing his find. "This is the best store!"

Guy had claimed the pick of the litter: his grandfather's tuxedo, which Averill Dapple Huber had worn to the Deering-Rant Black and Gold Cotillion of 1921, where he had met Guy's grandmother, then a hesitant fawn in white lace mitts, mitts which Venice had purchased a week ago, treasure even with half the pearl buttons missing.

The tux was seraphic. It was cut from that heavy, flat black wool, scorned in today's haberdashery in favor of dacrons and flimsier weaves; the jacket was double-breasted, with wide grosgrain lapels. The pants were extravagantly full and high-waisted, with thousands of pleats and knife-edge creases, all tapering to an anthemic break at the ankle, with a sag that defines the term "suavay." The tux was an engineering phenomenon. More fabric and fittings had been lavished on this single garment than on hundreds of contemporary models. Tuxes like Guy's justify the Depression; the wracking poverty, the sweatshop atrocity of the early rag trade are well honored. The tux had an indestructible slouch, a sweeping, almost Grecian contour. Tuxes ennoble men, they disguise every flaw and allow even the most petulant milquetoast to devastate. A man in a tux is an archetype; he becomes sculptural, a low, sleek black roadster, with chromium trim, in the moonlight.

It's perfect, Guy thought, in the cab on the way back to the loft. Now I have something to wear tonight! Guy cradled his tux, stroking it, running his fingers incestuously over the satin stripe on the trousers. There is a satisfaction that only superb clothing can offer, the joy of man raising himself from the mud, vindicating evolution. Life cannot lack purpose if a tuxedo exists—this is the obvious reply to the Samuel Beckett canon. Guy felt like a new mother, returning from the delivery room with her miracle. His bliss flowered into delirium as he discovered a moldering bag of M&M's in the tux's breast pocket. Guy nibbled his way home, imbued with history.

When Guy got in, Venice and Licky were both asleep, weary from sex, hair and the telephone. Naps are de rigueur among Manhattan youth, splitting the bustling preparation of the day from the blasé uproar of the night. From six until ten every evening, the better lofts, co-ops and hovels retain the calm of the nursery. Busy babies need their rest, their faces lush with cold cream or rigid with clay masque, their tummies audibly grinding the paté, Hunan or percodan of dinner, their body hair fended off via wax, bleach and tweezer, their dreams rampant with one another, fancies accompanied by the words ''never,'' ''darling'' and ''lower.'' Parents are pleased to discover their offspring asleep at these hours. They are unaware that this is mere prologue, that their children will soon rise and haunt the city till dawn and beyond.

Guy tiptoed in and hung his tuxedo in the bathroom, beside Licky's and Venice's outfits. He turned on the shower, allowing steam to billow about the assemblage, eliminating wrinkle and odor. He looked in the bedroom, where Licky and Venice were heaped on the bed. Guy didn't have the heart to wake them or to nudge Licky to the floor.

Guy scrubbed his face and took off his clothes. He hung a black velvet sleep mask, with a winking eye picked out in rhinestones, around his neck, and tiptoed back into the body of the loft. He lay down to sleep beside Danilo, sharing the dog's quilt and pillow. Guy noticed that Licky had partially cornrowed Danilo's fur, braiding it into a pleasing design, so that the dog wouldn't feel left out of the evening's conflagration.

As Guy began to drift off, he found he was looking forward to the evening. He was dozing on the precipice of adulthood. Would he plummet, would he glide, might he soar? What reward might arrive with imminent manliness—self-knowledge? backbone? a Master's Degree? something—and here Guy caught his breath, even as he slumbered—something with cashews in it?

10

Caronia

While the Huber contingent snoozed, the evening's gaiety began in earnest. Everywhere, men and women began to gargle, choose a scent and kiss the mirror, before setting out into the night. Throughout the city, social life crackled and then bonfired as the party circuit came to life.

Caronia Desti opened her evening at The Manhattan Museum of Larger Art. It was rumored that Caronia had died several years back but remained on Earth due to her unquenchable spirit and a calendar booked well into the year 2000. Indeed, at times Caronia seemed so physically fragile, so essentially weightless, that she could pass for a sequined helium, a shantung wisp of pure enthusiasm. Caronia was the essence of merriment, the distilled attar of a night on the town. Tonight she was to serve as Honorary Hostess of the annual benefit for The Cloak and Artifact Collection.

The Manhattan Museum of Larger Art is a great limestone pile, with limitless columns and broad granite plazas. The

Larger possesses that stately quality that so impresses school-children and later causes them to fidget. The Larger contains many of the globe's preeminent works, displayed in high marble halls with instructive labels. The Larger is where art goes to die.

The Cloak and Artifact Collection was assembled in an attempt to lure crowds back to the museum. It features the fashions of various historical epochs, repaired and slathered over mannequin forms. These exhibits are great fun, and museum-goers can learn much about their ancestors from inspecting their whalebone corsets and chain mail. The crowds pour in, mistaking the collection for a form of wholesale. Each year a gala heralds the compilation of a special exhibition, in tonight's instance an enchanting display of ancient footwear entitled "The Forbidden Tread: Shoes Of Imperial China."

Caronia had been busy for hours. The museum had been shuttered for the day, in preparation. Now hundreds of inadequate round tables and rented folding chairs filled the museum's Great Hall. Assistants flitted about, tufting a napkin, centering a piece of crystal or reviving a hyacinth. The Great Hall had a capacity of over five hundred guests, in configurations that had caused Caronia no end of tribulation. She had considered eliminating a seating plan altogether and letting the crowd joust for seats. Wouldn't it be mad, Caronia had thought, homesteading!

Caronia now stood at a balustrade on a terrace high above the Great Hall. Everything seemed in readiness. Caronia decided to enjoy a cigarette and watch the revelers arrive. For a moment, she felt a hostess's mild dread, that sincere desire for everyone to just go home. This will pass, Caronia told herself, as the early birds began to trickle in, the people who planned to hit the buffet, hit the bar and hit the hay. Humanity, Caronia thought, y'all come!

· · ·

The party, being a charity event, would attract few young people, who consider themselves charity events and see little cause
to share the wealth. The crowd would be that odious conglomer-
ate that passes for the Old Guard. The next to appear were the
Brunch Babies, the social succubi. These are women, Fighting
Fifty, with nothing better to do. They live for the splashier museum parties and dystrophy events. They are the embalming
fluid of Manhattan nightlife.

These women appear in the paper, and no one is quite sure
why. They dither about, co-chairing the committee, organizing
the luncheon, catching the Fall Line from spindly gilt chairs,
their black sunglasses poised atop their lacquered heads like
bats trapped in amber. These women do not want to work, they
want to keep busy. Fetish dieters, they attain the figures of El
Greco Christs, pinched and tucked and taut; they are the antith-
esis of sex. Intercourse might disturb the termites.

These women have husbands, Junior Partners and Vice-
Chairmen and such, diligent, golfing men whose thinning hair
is always exactly the color of their skin. These men are always
tired and never fun. They hate parties and are more than happy
to beg off. So the wives sprint on alone, or escorted by jowling
decorators. A wife and a homosexual are practically the true
Manhattan marriage. If a pair somehow mated, their offspring
would be an appointment book.

The Brunch Babies moved into the party, squealing and peck-
ing, as they had not seen each other since the afternoon.

"Tanzo, endless Tanzo!" Caronia called, spotting a familiar
face amid the WASPery. Caronia sailed down the steps to the
Great Hall and entered the crush. "Tanzo, the shoes, you must
see the shoes!" she told the Japanese designer. "They are not
for the feet, they are shoes of the cortex, of the medulla, of the
mind itself! They shall resurrect the toe! Yes! After tonight, we
shall have toes again!"

Caronia was like a feral child, raised in a sunless pit, for whom the world was ever vital and astonishing. Caronia spoke only in revelation, in seizure; she so wanted the world to amaze, to surpass the norm. Caronia led Tanzo off to inspect the exhibition. They inched through the crowd, and the party eddied about them.

"I do adore these things," said a Brunch Baby, adjusting a ruby. "It's so much nicer than a *disease*. You know they're not about to, you know, trot out anything on a *crutch*."

"My dear," the woman's companion replied, "last year I went to that Olympics, that Special Olympics, for the retarded, there they were, running, and swimming, and knocking things over. I told Harrison, 'This year, it's the Larger.' I don't like anything I have to meet."

With her great-aunt in tow, Lucy Yates Membrane swept past the Brunch Babies. "We start over here, Aunt Gretchen," said Lucy, motioning toward a canvas, "with the Titian."

Lucy had rented two cassette players and a series of "Masters of The Larger" cassettes at the Information Desk. Headsets allowed Lucy and Aunt Gretchen to roam the museum at will, barraged by lectures on the various urns and frescoes and forgeries. Lucy wore her cassette player slung from the sash of her gown, which was lemon tafeta with a rickrack tulip appliqué. Aunt Gretchen Dow Membrane was fond of Lucy, although at times her strapping niece seemed exasperatingly prim.

"This is fascinating, Aunt Gretchen. Did you know that Ramses II was entombed with his entire household?"

"Yes, dear. There was a time when service meant something in this country."

The Membrane women pushed on, neatly avoiding a squabble between two Captains of Industry in adjoining wheelchairs.

". . . and then Strap Deering went back, long, but he handed off to Carp Kettleberry, *ha!*"

"But what about '07—*that* was a game!"

" '07? '07? Wait—Punt Kepley? Ten all? 'Three-fingers' Kepley and the Hellhound Brigade!"

"The third quarter! Creeley, Hurd Meltmore's boy, and Petergitz out with a knee . . ."

The party, always over by midnight, was near peak. The Membrane women were smuggling daring thimblefuls of Beaujolais into the Pre-Hellenic Membrane Patio.

Contessa Larini was lecturing her sister on the foolhardiness of marrying heterosexuals ("Zey expect tings").

Alice Huber, in a nice long skirt-and-sweater set, encountered an old school chum, Mrs. Dorothy Wainmess, of the Museum Board. The ladies made the most of their reunion.

"Why, Diffy Wainmess, how *are* you? It's been too long, don't you look nice, is that a serape? Isn't this just lovely tonight, such a good group . . . Dick is well, the boys are blooming . . . Yes, even Guy, he's working hard, making us proud . . . Yes, he's engaged to someone, let me see, I believe it's Lucy Membrane, isn't that nice? I do admire the Membranes, always on the go . . . What? Why, the Membranes did have a son, Bayliss I believe; Irene says he was lost with the Peace Corps, somewhere in the Veldt . . . Now Diffy, how are Gray and the children? You know, I always loved that you married Gray Wainmess; I always thought you could name your babies Peach, and Coral . . . No, I do understand, other children can be so cruel . . . She did? Your Courtney? Under a train? Are you sure she didn't just lose something? I'm always under things—my keys, my compact, it's never-ending . . . No? Well, then I am sorry, what a shame . . . Was she unhappy?

"My . . . possessed by a demon? Well, that is something, and so close to her degree . . . Now, Diffy, stop that sobbing, don't make me sorry I asked . . . Diffy, who knows anymore? Young people—they all seem to be dancing now, isn't that what

I read? At that place? Our Guy traipsed in yesterday, hair as blue as blazes—I didn't ask . . . It's all just a phase, that's how I like to see things—Mr. Roosevelt, armpit hair, sex . . . Remember all that to-do in the Sixties? And that was nothing to worry about, now was it. One day I was repapering the guest bath on the Vineyard, and I just thought, Strawberries on lime, that was the Sixties, time for a change, up went a nice little Swiss dot on navy, and everything was fine . . . Sometimes a dried pod arrangement alone can make all the difference . . . Yes, I do worry about the drugs, one day I just sat our boys down, and I asked them if they were ever tempted. And I remember Guy spoke right up, he said, 'No, Mommy, never,' and he told me how much he liked my third eye. He's a good boy . . . Oh look, that Mrs. Desti is leaving . . . She's such a *vivid* woman, I could never wear that, but then I never would . . . Oh Diffy, hush, I would look perfectly awful . . ."

Caronia stepped gratefully into Tanzo Matta's limousine, parked outside the Larger. She took a deep breath, pleased to be free of her hostessing chores. All those people are far too at home in a museum, she decided.

"The Club de," Caronia told the chauffeur. "Let's skedaddle!"

11

First Night

Guy stood just inside the Club de's front door, compulsively smoothing his lapels and trying not to hyperventilate. It was nearly midnight and time for his shift to begin. He hoped he looked nice. He had examined himself in all sorts of things—a taxi's rear-view mirror, a puddle, the corneas of both coatcheck girls, acres of shop windows. At night, everything becomes reflective.

Venice had considered packing Guy a lunch before he left the loft, as a wifely gesture. She had located a tin lunchbox, embossed with cartoon characters, but she liked it so much that she decided to use it as an evening bag instead. Guy had slipped into his tuxedo, which he wore with a plain white T-shirt. Licky had picked up the zebra shoes earlier in the day, and when Guy stepped into them, his toes had wriggled in gratitude.

Waiting inside the Club, Guy trembled, shifting his body inside his terrific new clothes. Guy had slicked his hair back except his streak, which he teased into a feathered prominence, like a raven's wing.

Renzo, one of the Himalayan Mafia bouncers, shoved his skull into the Club, searching for Guy.

"Hey, where's da new one?" Renzo asked.

The bouncers were not Licky's sculpted Belvederes; they were immense, formless slag heaps of muscle. The bouncers would plant themselves before the Club, immovable and unseeing. They each checked in at almost three hundred pounds, mostly neck. The bouncers began the day with breakfasts of steak and dozens of eggs, they spoke of "keepin' their weight up" and "beefin' it." Their eyes peered out from beneath Neanderthal overhangs, and they shaved their heads, plotting a studied brutality, an unreachable grossness. These were men whose heroes were minerals.

"I'm Guy," Guy told Renzo. "Hi, I'm the new one!"

"Yo," said Carmine, the other bouncer, the one with the eyepatch. He held the door open and said, "Get out here."

Guy decided to befriend the bouncers, he wondered if he should toss field mice into their cages. The bouncers were indispensable; in the event of gunplay, Guy could duck behind one. Guy was certain that bullets could penetrate a good deal of Renzo or Carmine without causing substantial damage; he could imagine the bouncers' bodies in cross-section, the projectile slowed and halted somewhere within a forearm or chin.

"Hey, guys," said Guy, "here I come!"

Guy, readying himself, took a deep breath. A bit of panic set in, and he turned, heading back into the Club. Renzo's hand grabbed Guy by the nape of his neck, and Guy found himself outside the Club.

"Dis is Guy," said Renzo, to Carmine.

"Yo," said Carmine. "How ya doin'."

"Hi," said Guy, regaining his balance. He stared at his feet, realizing he now stood within the sacred rectangle, the holy zone bounded by aluminum stanchions and worn red velvet ropes. Here I am, thought Guy.

"I'm fine," Guy said aloud, still examining his shoes and the concrete around them.

Gradually, careful not to sprain anything, Guy looked up. He squinted, caught by the white glare of the photographers' arc lights, arranged for both tabloid stills and television cameras. Then Guy looked beyond this brilliant, not unpleasant nimbus, and he saw the crowd. Boy, Guy thought, look at *that!*

Guy had never been on this side of things before; he'd never stared directly into the jaws of the famished behemoth. There they were—the hundreds of faces, the fun seekers, the supplicants, the huddled masses, the people who wanted to get in. Guy's stare was innocent, entranced, that of an infant at his first birthday party, too young to know what a birthday party was but dizzy from the fuss. The silent crowd was aware that a new door had come on duty.

"Hi," said Guy, to the mob, shyly.

"HI," said the mob, everyone trying to sound as fabulous as possible.

"How are you?" asked Guy, who had not been brought up in a barn.

"FINE," the mob replied.

Pleasantries exchanged, Guy kept looking, mesmerized. He saw the smiles, the flecks of sweat, the wilting hairstyles, the clothing stiff from the hanger. He smelled the musky cologne, the virile aftershave, the medicinal breath spray. Guy felt like the lone Jesuit they send out each morning to unlatch the gate at Lourdes. He felt he should have a starter's pistol.

And then it began. The bubble of yearning burst. The polite silence would not hold, and the crowd detonated.

"I LOVE YOU, GUY!" yelled a dermatologist's wife, who had read of Guy's new position in the morning paper.

"I *want* you, Guy," whispered a stewardess, reaching out to stroke Guy's tuxedo.

"Boy," said Guy to Carmine, "aren't they great?"

"GUY, LOOK—LITTLE GUY!" shouted a flushed woman in a hospital gown, hoisting an hours-old baby high above her head. "I NAMED HIM GUY!"

"Thanks!" said Guy, honored.

"HEY, JERK! LEMME IN!" demanded a beefy college linebacker, who had been waiting for three hours with the rest of his team. These jocks began a chant, waving baseball bats and bellowing "JERK! JERK! JERK!"

Guy shook an impish finger at these fellows, who lunged at him but were devoured by the crush.

"Three, Guy!" said an Entertainment Lawyer, offering folded cash. Entertainment Lawyers do not really want to practice law; they want to meet Ratallia Parv. Guy wondered if Entertainment Medicine would be next, for doctors who wished to operate solely on celebrities.

"ONE HUNDRED AND FIFTY-SIX, GUY! MISS MIPPY AND GRADES FOUR THROUGH EIGHT!"

"Guy! Guy, darlingest, you know *me,* from Brett and Erica's, in Amagansett, that divine weekend, the potato sack race, the *endive!* Isn't this *silly?* Isn't it totally *ridic?* Guy, it's Marisa!"

"GUY, PLEEEEEEZE, JUST PLEEEEEEEEEZE, OH PLEEEEEEEEEEEEZE, I'LL BE YOUR BEST FRIEND! WE'LL GO PLACES AND TALK ON THE PHONE AND WEAR MATCHING OUTFITS TO HOMECOMING GAMES!"

"Guy, I'm a friend of your folks, and this is Mrs. Meertop. When you were, oh, just a pup, we used to come by and read to you. Mrs. Meertop rubbed Petroleum jelly on your little tummy! I remember we gave you a Funny Mr. Potatohead gizmo, how you laughed! You were a dear child, always our favorite. Guy, let me in and you can HAVE HER!"

"LISTEN TO THE MAN!" said Mrs. Meertop, her silver wig falling rakishly over one eye.

"Hi, Mrs. Meertop!" said Guy, waving.

"Look at me, Guy—can you feel it too? It's eerie, isn't it? We're sharing a, what would you call it, a dynamic exchange, I know you, you know me, maybe from Rome, or Carthage. I was the Consul of Ethiopia; you were a concubine then . . ."

"OH MY GOD, HE IS SO CUTE, EVEN IF HE WASN'T THE DOOR! HI, GUY! IT'S ME! IT'S LEONARDA! LEONARDA LADURCCA!"

"Anybody?" asked Carmine, barely glancing at the mob as he stood with his paws behind his back, at parade rest. Carmine's fingers twitched hungrily, longing for a spine or ankle to wrench and send skyward. To his credit, Carmine was very good with children. He often kept his little daughter tucked safely behind his ear, like a cigarette.

"What?" said Guy, mesmerized by the throng.

"Anybody?" Carmine repeated, giving Guy a friendly knock on the head.

"Oh," said Guy, rubbing his head. Oh my God, he thought. I have to choose. I work here. This is my job! But which ones? Guy scanned the crowd frantically, searching for clues. Should I let everybody in, he wondered. Nobody?

Guy knew he shouldn't let everyone in. Compassionate as that might be, the management would frown. And besides, Guy would be trampled. If I don't let anyone in, Guy reasoned, then the Club would be really exclusive. And broke, he realized.

An unaccustomed anxiety rose in Guy's soul. He felt as if he had swallowed a large steel ball-bearing, with spikes. His arms went numb, hanging frozen at his sides. His feet were welded to the sidewalk. Guy grew paralyzed with social responsibility. Could I come back tomorrow night? he wanted to scream. Could I take a training course? Can I just close my eyes and point? Just as he was about to black out, the Lord smiled.

Guy saw Oded Ben Fadood and two of his wives approaching the rope.

Hallelujah, Guy thought. Oded! The sheik was a sure bet. He was unimaginably wealthy, and freakish on an international scale. The multiple wives in their signature black lent him cachet, even trendsetter status (*Glaze* was already planning a cover on "The New Polygamy").

"Three!" Guy called out happily, motioning Renzo to open the rope. Oded trotted past Guy, his head nodding within his hooded burnoose. Oded seemed unusually tall, but Guy assigned the change to healthy American meals.

"Nummy lummy num num num," said Oded, which Guy took for an Arabic thank-you. Guy made a jovial "OK" sign with his thumb and forefinger.

"Hi!" said Guy, with a crisp salute. "Anytime!" Guy wanted to appear efficient, like those helpful gas-station attendants in the TV commercials, who checked the oil and the tires without being asked.

"Tree," said Renzo, ushering Fadood and Co. into the Club. Renzo wondered why Oded had only brought two wives with him this evening. Maybe he got the other ones chained inna basement, Renzo thought, or maybe they're atta beauty parlor. I wonda what them chickies wear under allat black crapola.

Renzo, it may be assumed, never held any one thought for very long.

"Whoooo," Guy exhaled, as the door shut behind the bustling nomads. Guy was so relieved. I guess I'm starting to get the hang of things, he thought. Oded! All right! Okey-doke, here we go. He shook out his hands, limbering up. He snapped his fingers and put on his sunglasses.

"We're rollin'!" he said to Renzo.

"GUYYYYY! LOOK—WHEN I CLOSE MY EYES YOU CAN SEE IT, RIGHT ON THE LID: G-U-Y! IT'S PERMANENT!"

"Dwayne Fencer, Guy, ABC News Nightliners. We understand this is your first night out here. Could you tell us, in your
own words, how it all feels, first time solo at America's *numero
uno* nightspot, where the Beautiful People meet the Jet Set, and
anything and everything goes!"

"Gee," said Guy, into the microphone. He looked into the
camera. "Hi, everybody!" he said. "Come on down!"

"Guy, I'm a rilly, rilly good dancer, Hustle, Latin Hustle, the
Bump, Double Bump, Freeport Lock, Freeport Lock with Varia-
tions, Needlenose Drytickle, Rockdown Bleedbustle, Rockdown
Bleedbustle with Dips—"

"Guy, Dwayne Fencer again. You look great, if we could just
get a little bit of film inside the Club . . ."

"COME ON, EVERYBODY! LET'S ALL SING! GUY, ISN'T
THAT A GOOD IDEA? WE'LL ALL SING, AND THEN
WE'LL ALL GO IN!"

A bus of Fundamentalist pickets arrived and were comman-
deered to stack bodies and match wandering toddlers to distracted parents. A hand grenade was tossed, but Carmine
chucked it back into the crowd, where it exploded without
maiming any real possibilities.

The street vendors replenished their tins of suicide pel-
lets, which they sold alongside heart-shaped silver balloons
that read "New York, New York—So Nice They Named It
Twice."

"Ya wanna balloon?" a vendor asked Guy.

"Sure!" said Guy.

As Guy took the balloon, he was caught by the glint of a diamond earring. The earring was worn by a young lady lolling
on the roof of a limousine far out in the street. She was poured
into a strapless black sheath. She sat with her legs crossed, and
her head back. She was gazing idly into the night sky, her
blonde hair falling onto her shoulders.

The young lady was world class, insanely oblivious. She appeared to be moonbathing on some private terrace. She held a cigarette in one gloved hand. She brought the cigarette to her lips, and inhaled.

Guy stared at this careless vision, his chin lodged firmly on his chest. His balloon soared skyward.

Then Guy caught himself. I'm on duty, he realized. I have a job to do! That girl is so gorgeous, I would kill for that girl, but is she . . . de? Is she the grace note the symphony demands? Who does she know? Who are her people? Whose list is she on? What would she add, what inescapable fizz, what absolute plus? Did the Club require her presence? Would the Club suffer without her particular sheen? Was she a definite yes? Just who was she?

"Darling," the young lady mouthed, and the limousine's driver gunned the engine, impatient to get moving.

"Venice!" Guy cried, delighted, and then, turning to Renzo, "One please!"

Renzo waded into the mob, cleaving the waters and a face or two. He slogged his way out to where Venice dallied. Renzo was grateful for his years in the swamps of Thailand with the Green Berets, smashing crocodiles and saboteurs. Those were nothing compared to a girl from Flatbush with a nail file.

Renzo lifted Venice to his shoulder, like a circus strongman, and hiked back through the crowd. Venice waved gaily to the hordes below, gouging attackers with her six-inch heels. Venice felt like one of those religious statues carried through the streets of small Italian villages on saint's days. If she recalled correctly, the crowd should be showering her with scraps of colored paper; no one did. "Hi, darlings," Venice called to the crowd, as she pitched and swayed. "Get with it!"

Renzo deposited Venice behind the rope. She stood back from Guy, studying him. Then she grabbed him by the lapels and kissed him passionately.

"You're working!" Venice said, still holding Guy's lapels, "I'm dying!"

"WHO IS THAT WHORE?" someone screamed from the crowd. "HEY, BUBBLES!"

Bubbles? Guy recognized his childhood nickname, invented when his friends had discovered the source of his trust fund. Guy had never been overtly fond of the nickname, so his schoolmates had hurled it without pause. The name had eventually found its way onto all of Guy's diplomas. Guy checked the crowd to find who had revived his torment.

"Licky!" said Guy. "Renzo, one please—the one in the net stockings!"

Licky had chosen to honor Guy by appearing as a saucy French maid, in a brief, petticoated, black satin uniform with a lacy white apron, heels and a little starched cap. Licky had long abandoned gender as a restriction in wardrobe selection; why miss out on half the world's couture? Licky considered all the world his stage, and all clothing merely costume. This evening he had decided against a wig, marcelling his own hair instead in a daring, mannish style.

Renzo refused to fetch Licky, who frightened him. He suspected that Licky was the only person in the world who could beat him up; Renzo would admit defeat in a second rather than get tickled. Licky was left to fight his way through the pack, biting and poking. He finally climbed atop a public-school civics instructor and dove for the space behind the rope.

"You're working!" said Licky, picking himself up off the ground and hiking his girdle back into place. "Oh, Monsieur Huber!"

Guy, Venice and Licky looked at each other, breathless. They'd reached the raft, they were together, and the night was in its infancy.

"Renzo," said Guy, "can you take it for a minute? I just want to go in for a second, with these guys, is that okay?"

"You got it," said Renzo, benevolently. The kid had done good, and Renzo wanted that guy in the dress to get moving.

"Take a break," Renzo told Guy, and to Venice, "Hiya, cupcake!"

"*Caro,*" Venice growled. "Ooooh . . ."

"Oh, *Renzo,*" said Licky as he rustled by, "oo-la-la!"

"GUYYYYYYY!" screamed the mob as Guy and his cronies slipped into the Club. "GUY, COME BACK! WE LOVE YOU!"

"Darlings, really," Venice said to the raucous multitude as the door hissed shut behind her. "He's married!"

12

The Brawl

Guy, Venice and Licky ran through the lobby, boomeranging off the mirrored walls. They were gleeful over Guy's success and more than ready to dance. They could hear the music, the Club's infectious pulse, and they were all having a hard time standing still.

"Guys, this is too bizarre," said Guy, swinging on a palm tree. "My job is really easy! I just got out there, right, and I thought I was going to hemorrhage, but it was fine! I just sort of did it! Well, I mean, it's not really easy, and I was going to ask if I could bring out a chair or something, I mean, when I think about it I get exhausted, but I did it!"

"But jais," said Venice, her shoulders swaying to the music.

"You're a door," Licky said, "a style sheriff! The taste police!"

"I know," said Guy, with a pang of conscience. "It's disgusting, isn't it?"

"It's a dirty job," said Licky. "You should be ashamed."

"Licky!" Guy protested. "You got me this job!"

"I know," said Licky, giggling, and running on ahead.

"Darling," said Venice, putting her arm around Guy, "don't worry."

"Really?" said Guy, concerned.

"Really," said Venice, "you were going to hell anyway."

As the trio entered the body of the Club, they encountered a scene of social rapture—Caronia Desti greeting Sheik Fadood.

"Oded!" Caronia cried. "Oded Ben Fadood, my sheik, my pasha, my indefatigable Moslem! Sound the koan!"

Caronia threw her reedy limbs around her favorite barbarian. Caronia had long favored Fadood, certain that only in the sheik's parched, oil-rich corner of the Third World was the veil truly appreciated. Caronia lifted the hood of Oded's burnoose, plunging into the folds of mottled linen, seeking the smoldering orbs and fetid, lightly salted moustache she so adored. Caronia, it must be recalled, was a woman of diverse passions. She relished all experience and had once shot a fashion spread on Death Row, a layout she called "Last Looks."

"Infidel!" Caronia howled, drawing back in horror. These were not Fadood's smoldering orbs! This was not Fadood's moustache! This was not any breed of potentate!

"Who are you?" Caronia demanded, aghast at the cruel deception, *"and what have you done with Fadood?"*

For a few hideous, free-falling seconds, Debbie tried to conceal her ruse, clutching her disguise about herself. Debbie had fashioned the burnoose from her mother's caftan, and a fitted sheet from Wamsutta's "Chic of Araby" Collection. She had accessorized with her beagle's leash and a batch of those golden-toned chainlink belts so popular in the go-go boot era.

Debbie shook her hips furiously, hoping her belts would be found suitably Persian. Her face was smeared with a quick-tanning lotion, an orange ooze which now decorated Caronia's cheeks as well. Debbie pulled a tube of the lotion from a pocket and attempted to replenish the effect, desperate to achieve a semblance of foreign flesh.

"But . . . but . . ." Debbie sputtered, searching for an Arabic phrase.

"I toldja it wasn't gonna work," said Michelle matter-of-factly. Michelle tugged the black gauze from her face. Michelle's masquerade consisted of a Cub Scout pup tent, which Michelle had soaked in a washtub of black dye for several days. Debbie had performed all the necessary stitching in her high-school home economics class, where she claimed to be sewing a poncho.

"Fuck, this is so *embarrassing*," said Bruce, ripping off his own makeshift chador (created from equal parts bedspread and shower curtain). Bruce was glad to be rid of this cumbersome costume. What if one of the guys saw him, dressed like some fucking Arab chick? Bruce had only agreed to the scam due to certain promises on Debbie's behalf, promises involving local motels and panties with racy slogans. Bruce had wanted to impersonate Fadood, but Debbie, having a more natural moustache, had insisted otherwise.

"But we got IN!" shrieked Debbie. "Leave us alone!"

"Oh my God," said Licky, investigating the situation, and Caronia's screams, "it's Jersey!"

"Hey," said Guy, impressed, "you're not Oded."

"Darlings," said Venice. "You sly things."

"What's goin' on?" asked Carmine, summoned by a busboy. "What is this shit?"

"LEAVE ME ALONE!" screamed Debbie. Debbie's burnoose now gaped wildly, revealing an almost new puffed-sleeve dacron party dress in powder blue with a print of tiny smiling lurex faces. "I'M IN!"

"Jeez," said Carmine, hefting a squalling Michelle under his

arm. "People is always doin' this. Tryin' to get in, screamin'
they know somebody—real bush."

"It wasin't *my* idea!" protested Michelle, about to sink her
molars into Carmine's thigh. "I wannid to go to my friend Janice
Pitterman's house, we were gonna put snot on our fingers and
chase her little brother!"

"Yeeeeouch!" said Carmine, as Michelle's teeth found their
mark. "Don't you put no snot on me!"

"Deb, I told you this was fuckin' looneytunes," said Bruce,
as Renzo approached. Bruce assumed a karate stance, dimly recalled from a Banzai Protection men's deodorant commercial.
"Hey, buddy," he told Renzo, "you touch me, you lose a fuckin'
arm!"

"I'M IN! I'M IN!" Debbie screeched, as Carmine chased her
around the bar. The bartenders thoroughly enjoyed the fracas
and shot jets of soda water at anyone who came near.

"Whoa!" said a bartender, squirting Renzo. "Go for it!"

"Hey, dude," said another bartender to Bruce, "think
quick!"

"Keep your distance, buddy. I'm tellin' ya, keep your fuckin'
distance," Bruce warned Renzo. Then he tripped, as his Manuel
Elegante running shoes, twelve pounds of latex and canvas, became hopelessly entangled in his fallen chador.

"Darlings, he's *heaven,*" said Licky, always a sucker for anything retrograde. "Darling," he repeated, drawing up beside
Bruce, "you are *bliss.*"

"Who the fuck are you, lady?" said Bruce, trying not to di-
vide his attention as Renzo advanced.

"Hey, punk," said Renzo, foam filling the corners of his lips,
"which side ya part your face on?"

"Don't you love it?" Licky trilled, as bloodshed seemed imminent. "This is the way straight men have sex!"

"HAIIIIIIII-YA!" yelled Bruce, bringing the side of his hand down onto Renzo's neck. His hand immediately crumpled. Renzo took little notice and tossed Bruce, flailing and cursing, over his shoulder.

"I'm warnin' ya, pisshead!" Bruce swore. "I know PRES-SURE POINTS!"

"Brucie, SHUT UP!" screamed Debbie, now immobilized in Carmine's hammerlock. "PLEASE, LEMME GO! I'M IN! I GOT IN!"

"Snot!" howled Michelle, as Carmine used his free arm to drag her out by the hair. "I GOT SNOT ON MY FINGER!"

"NOOOOOOOOOOOOO!!!!!" Debbie moaned, with the stark terror of an animal separated from her young, with the wail of a martyred she-thing. "PRETTY PLEEEEEEEZE!"

"My dears," said Caronia, recovering her power of speech, "who were they? Saboteurs! *Provocative!*"

"Great action!" said the bartenders, pouring beer on each other's heads.

"Weren't they mad?" said Licky, smoothing his apron. "Don't you just love it? I mean, *Martians?*"

"Too hot," said Venice, seated on the bar.

"I feel really dumb," said Guy. "I mean, I let them in, my first night on the job. I'm such a cheesehole. But that was great!"

13

Most Visible Couple

Debbie, Bruce and Michelle were carted out. Order was restored, much to everyone's disappointment. Licky ran off toward the disc jockey's booth. Licky wanted to encourage the
disc jockey to play his favorite song, something about a boogie
doctor offering "hot love injections."

The music at the Club de was geared for primal movement.
It was all beat, all tireless, insinuating wham. The volume was
diabolical, so loud that the dancers felt swallowed by the ele-
mental bass line. The music became almost solid, a wall of
pound. The instruments employed on the most popular records
were electric machines that could be programmed to imitate traditional instruments or to produce new noises, nitro-blasts and
machine-gun stutters and impossible echoes.

The music was pure orgasm, irresistible, aimed at the pelvis.
Hips would not rest, the music beckoned on the most basic, hor-
monal level. The lyrics, when audible, invariably told tales of

a black woman's love troubles, expressed in moans and sizzles. The disc jockeys teased the dancers with scraps of favorite numbers, until people were screaming in frustration. Finally, the song of the moment was tossed on the turntable, and the dance floor jammed. The disc jockeys fiddled with the song, repeating phrases, overdubbing, twisting the rhythm until strong men wept and strong women laughed at them.

People danced alone or in packs but rarely with a single partner. People lost themselves in the music and danced with the world. The dancers shut their eyes and moved their limbs in churning, athletic patterns. There were good dancers, lithe and spinning; self-conscious dancers, limited to small, boxy movements; and there were always a few stockbrokers, their neckties knotted around their foreheads, men who had no idea what to do with their bodies away from a computer terminal or a squash racquet.

The best dancers put themselves at the music's mercy, allowing it to pummel them. The dancing at the Club de was not romantic but sexual. In a ballroom, the dancers experience ritual and intrigue and politesse, with all emotion masked by the foxtrot or minuet. At the Club de, the dancers reached for release and sweat.

Guy and Venice made their way to the catwalk as the music began to percolate (the best songs did not arrive until the evening was well under way). They scrambled up the stair and soon stood side by side at the catwalk's railing. They were proprietary, now that Guy was on staff, admirals rather than passengers aboard the listing Cunard. They did not speak, due to the music, but there was no need to. They were happy.

Guy knew that Venice loved him because when it was just the two of them, she never called him "darling." As for Venice, men had offered her sportscars and Arabian stallions, movie roles and weekends outside Gstaad. But no one had ever dyed their hair blue for her. Together the Hubers shared a tidy cottage of devotion amidst a steaming jungle of pleasure.

Facing one another, Guy and Venice began to dance. Venice, in her molded dress, could not make any large movements. She stayed almost still, using only her bare shoulders and the swing of her hair. She kept her head back and her eyes half-closed. The effect was intoxicating, as if Venice were wriggling out of her clothing, inch by inch.

Guy loved to dance. Dancing is the opposite of working. Guy was a very good dancer, full of high spirits and abandon. Sometimes he would make faces as he danced, scrunching his features in time with the music. This was not really cool, but Guy did it anyway. His hair became damp and his blue streak fell over one eye, looking very Elvis.

Guy and Venice surrendered their bodies to the disc jockey's whim. The music poured through them, until they couldn't take it one more second. Simultaneously, they opened their eyes.

"Guy," said Venice, still dancing, her eyes shining, her voice lascivious with scheme.

"What?" asked Guy, eagerly.

"Everyone's watching," Venice said, and, with superb violence, she grabbed Guy and began kissing him.

From below, the gossip rose like fresh bread, fragrant and steaming. Guy and Venice were the town topic, truly one of the Ten Most Visible Couples.

"Baron, look—Venice and Guy Huber," said a baking-soda heiress. "Too amusant . . . too faboo . . . isn't she? Sad . . . they've been living apart. It's all a ruse. He's really with that little starlet, the Hungarian with the nipples, and she's with my husband—they have an apartment on Lower Fifth, full of, you know, *posters.* My husband—he claims he's keeping some girl he found outside of Cairo, as a slave, but I'm not a fool. No one can keep a slave in the city anymore."

.   .   .

"Why did he do that to his hair?" wondered a documentary filmmaker. "It's the purest ugh. Do you think they really take those injections for their skin—you know, sheep fetuses or something?"

"Sheep fetuses?" inquired the filmmaker's swain.

"Of course, they liquefy them, they puree the placenta, and it gives you a glow. I'm sure if you see either of them in daylight it's tragic beyond words. I hear he's totally broke, they're living in a *trailer.* "

"I dunt lick her," announced Ratallia. "Che is holdink him. I vud mek him heppy. I vud be larch vid his childt. I must haf childt, to be vuman, ant my cluck, ju know, de vuman's cluck, is tickink, in my voomb. I vill mek pikchur about dis, de vuman choosink betveen career ant childt, is so importunt. I haf childt somvere, dey vill nut let me see it. Vait, let me svitch nose-trulls."

"Well, I'm bored," said Licky, traipsing onto the catwalk. Licky had been dancing below, his petticoats flying. Licky was a most accomplished dancer. He could indulge in the most frenzied gyrations while holding a cigarette aloft.

Guy and Venice broke their clinch.

"Darling," Venice told Guy, fixing his hair, "you've worked hard enough."

"Boy, I sure have," said Guy, wiping his brow. A job, he thought, it does take it out of you. And they had so much more to do tonight.

"Where to?" asked Guy.

"Quo vadis?" replied Venice.

14

Mistake #2

Guy, Venice and Licky collected their coats. They headed through the lobby, discussing the evening's options and modes of transportation.

"Carmine, we're going," said Guy as they hit the evening air, and Guy's name was heard from a thousand shivering lips. "Can you take it for a while? Another guy'll be here for the late shift, is that okay?"

"Is that okay, Carmine?" Venice repeated, stroking Carmine's cheek. "You big honeybunch."

"No prob," said Carmine, and to Guy, "She'll bury ya."

"Ya did A-okay," Renzo told Guy.

"Call me," said Venice to Renzo.

"Lunch," said Licky to Carmine.

"Thanks, you guys," Guy told the bouncers. "You're terrific!"

·   ·   ·

As this leavetaking continued, an agonizingly elongated car pulled up in front of the Club. A shrouded Bedouin emerged, followed by six docile women in black gauze and sunglasses. With the assistance of bodyguards, this group made their way toward the red velvet rope.

"Uh-oh," said Guy, noticing the platoon's approach.

"Hi, Jersey!" Licky said. "I call it brave."

"Hit the road, ya geeks," said Renzo. "Dontcha ever learn?"

"Darlings," said Venice, "this must've cost you a mint."

Venice playfully lifted one of the women's veils, and said "Peekaboo." The woman shrieked and was set upon and blinded by her fellow wives.

"Oh, dear," said Licky. "College girls."

"I am invite," said the hooded figure, attempting to push past the rope. "You are not with the understanding."

"I'm with the understandin', bozo," said Renzo, cracking his knuckles in anticipation. "I'm understandin' you are some dumb turd."

"I am being Fadood!" said the shocked primitive, drawing himself up to his full five feet, two inches.

"He is being Fadood!" said Hassad, trying to recall where he'd left his bullwhip.

"He is bein' bullshit," said Renzo, and the mountain came to Mohammed, hurling him half a block. Carmine caught Hassad by his narrow sharkskin lapels and sent him soaring after his employer.

"Oh my, my," said Ramira. "This is being the excitement!"

"Hips, hips hooray!" yelled Hofstra.

"Partieeeeee!" screamed Salima, and the wives ran ecstatically into the night, in all directions, like billiard balls released by the cue ball's tap. Only Tira paused for a split-second, to ask Licky about his eyelashes.

"Lissen. They come back, I'm breakin' fingers," warned Carmine.

"Hey," said Renzo, petulant. "Ya said I could do the next fingers."

"Who *is* she?" asked Licky, standing on tiptoe to watch the crumpled Fadood pulling himself up to the sidewalk.

"Poor babies," said Venice.

"Are you guys okay?" Guy asked Renzo and Carmine.

"We're just warmin' up," replied Carmine.

"I worry about you," said Guy. "This place is crazy."

"BYE, BUBBLES!" the crowd howled, as Guy and his friends departed.

"Hassad, you are to be calling the policing ones," commanded Oded Ben Fadood, as he limped into his limousine. He dabbed the blood from his lip with the hem of his shredded burnoose. "And you are to be calling the Mayor person, and the bigger ones."

"I will be doing this," said Hassad, reaching for the car's housephone. "Where are the wives being?"

"I am not with the knowing," said Fadood, fuming, "They are with the running off! I am saying, 'Hassad, we are to be bringing the camel rope, and the items of restraining,' and you are saying, 'Oh no, not to America. Why be carrying them? We can be buying the new ones on Fifth Avenue.' Where are the wives being, Hassad? *You* are to be telling *me!*"

"This is being no problem," said Hassad evenly, turning to the chauffeur. "Driving person, you are to be taking us to the downtown. We will be finding the wives, and we will be buying the items of restraining."

"Whereabouts, buddy?" asked the chauffeur.

"Macy's," said Hassad.

15

Quo Vadis

Guy, Venice and Licky tossed themselves into Venice's borrowed limousine, which had pulled up outside the Club. Everyone knew that renting a limousine was indisputably tacky; and owning a limo was such a bother, with the parking and all. Borrowing a limo seemed the thing to do.

The trio made small mewing sounds, swaddling themselves in the limo's mink lap robe. Guy adored limos; this was a *nouveau* passion, but he could not help himself. There is something splendidly criblike about limos, something sweet-smelling and protective. Being driven is the next best thing to being carried. Guy especially liked the most vulgar, custom-made stretch limos, like Fadood's, which were true pleasure units. Limousines are the final remnant of the sedan chair in Western culture.

"I love limos," said Guy, squeezing Venice under the lap robe.

"I love chauffeurs," said Venice, squeezing him back.

"No taste," said Licky, "either of you." Then he switched on the color TV and fixed himself a daiquiri at the bar.

After touring for a bit, Licky directed the driver to Solitary, an after-hours club for sadomasochists which Licky hoped to popularize. Solitary is located on the waterfront, in the meat-packing district.

The group entered the club through a door marked by a small barred window, hung with an enema bag as a seasonal wreath.

"An enema bag!" Licky remarked enthusiastically. "My hat is *off!*"

The club was large and surprisingly bright. The walls were covered with a flimsy walnut paneling, for a rec-room feeling. There was a gleaming porcelain trough set in the floor, and a set of rough-hewn stocks stood on a raised dais in the center of the room. A batch of rings and clamps hung on chains from the ceiling. A pegboard-lined wall offered a comprehensive library of whips and gags and lubricants. "Isn't it heaven?" Licky chirped, inspecting the pegboard. "Just like aquarium supplies!"

"I'm holding my tongue," said Venice, holding a fourteen-inch latex tongue.

"Boy, is this a hat?" asked Guy, balancing a rubber suction device on his head. Guy looked up as the club's membership began to trickle in.

"Oh dear," said Licky, as the regulars trotted over for a chat. "Trouble in Tahiti."

Solitary, it became apparent, catered to actual bondage aficionados, people from Bensonhurst and Perth Amboy, rather than the dream studs and towering dominatrixes Licky had envisioned. The people at Solitary were portly and jovial. They had met through folksy magazine ads, with captions like "Hi! We're

Janet and Ed!" The members would spend an evening flogging one another and then return home in station wagons whose bumpers boasted "We've Seen the Luray Caverns."

"Hiya," said one of the club's officers, an aluminum-siding salesman by day. Tonight he wore a leather executioner's hood, a pair of studded chaps, and a twenty-function digital watch. "I'm Marv Winkler," he said, extending his hand, "and this is Denise."

"Hiya," said Denise. She was a blowzy hausfrau in chain mail bra, crotchless panties and a neck brace. "It's kinda slow tonight," Denise explained. "Wally's not here, and Connie couldn't get a sitter."

"Gee, who's Wally?" asked Guy.

"Oh, you'd love him," Denise replied, scratching a mosquito bite with the head of a veined Rover's Reamer dildo. "He makes this Jell-O mold, but with lotsa beer so we can, you know, pee on him after the buffet."

"Wally's a lotta laughs," said Marv, hoisting his leather codpiece. "Connie, ya didn't miss much. She just likes to make guys wear wigs. It's real boring, sometimes she pulls 'em off and they cry, but mostly it's just guys in wigs. I mean, who cares?"

"Marv don't mean it," Denise said quickly. "Connie's a great lady. We're gonna have, like, a day-care place out front so she can come more. Us girls gotta stick together," Denise told Venice. "Right, doll?"

"I love your neck brace," said Venice. "I wish I had the nerve."

"Oh, this ain't part of my, you know, ensemble," Denise replied, horrified. "I threw my back out in my aerobics class. That stuff is dangerous."

"Pathetic," Licky grunted. He stared at a team of accountants, nude except for dog collars and buckled chastity belts

worn about their loins. These men were being walked on all
fours, on lengths of rawhide attached to their collars. They were
tethered to a tiny woman wearing a navy double-knit pantsuit
and oversize eyeglasses on a safety-chain. A charm bracelet tin-
kled on her wrist; each charm was a gold replica of a grandchild's profile.

"Have you been eating?" the woman demanded of her
hounds. "Why don't you call?"

"We're sorry, Mistress," the accountants bayed. They were
rewarded with Puppy Chow and warm sweaters.

"This is all wrong," said Licky, hideously disillusioned. "It's
so . . . barbecue . . . so Arbor Day. The word is dowdy."

"I guess so," said Guy, "but it's kind of sweet. I mean, everyone should have a hobby."

"Quo vadis?" demanded Venice, putting out her cigarette on
someone's ear. "Triple quo vadis."

Whenever Venice said "Quo vadis?" it was a sign of near-
terminal Debutante's Dilemma, that crippler of young adults,
that refusal to accept the dawn, that demand for night-
prolonging narcotics, that insistence on sunglasses even in the
dimmest pit, that acute inability to go home. People hated to
get in before noon—it looked so sensible, so chicken, so gain-
fully employed. Over the years, staying out late had become an
endurance trial. The thirst for fun is unslakable, and no one
wants to be the first casualty, the person who calls a halt, the
person who makes up an excuse about an early morning appointment. Venice often boasted of forgetting her address, and
Licky liked to claim he had not been home since 1982.

Guy, Venice and Licky arrived at the Forty-second Street Utopia, a trucker's diner, as the sun came up. The diner was classic
Americana, an Eisenhower showroom of flecked formica, coffee

urns and rotating pie displays. The group sat on aluminum stools at the counter and chatted with additional rubble from the evening's hot spots.

"Where have you been?" a partygoer asked.

"Gee, everywhere," said Guy. "All over the place."

"Weren't you on the door tonight?" asked someone else, "at the Club de?"

"Uh-huh," said Guy modestly, nibbling on a piece of French toast, "it was my first night!"

"He was fabulous," said Venice proudly, draping her arm on Guy's shoulder. "People *hated* him."

"Was there really a massacre there," someone asked, "with fistfights and bodies and machine guns and things?"

"Not to my knowledge," said Licky, holding a Frosted Flake up to his ear, as jewelry. "I mean it was fun, but not *that* much fun."

The truckdrivers overheard this conversation and expressed their scorn by tossing lighted matches at Guy and his crowd.

"I'm full," said Guy, picking a match out of his hair.

"You brutes," Licky told the truckdrivers, "you're just shy. I'm in the book."

Guy, Venice and Licky left the diner. They headed for an after-after-hours club they had heard whispers of, said to exist in an abandoned gas station at the very tip of Manhattan Island.

They located the gas station, and climbed in through a broken window. They sat on the lube rack for almost an hour, watching the shadows desert the rotting fan-belt display. Venice fixed her lips, using a hubcap as a mirror. Guy toyed with the maps Licky had discovered in the adjoining office. Guy studied Ohio, trying to figure out where the top nightlife might be in the Buckeye State.

Licky finished folding the Rhode Island Turnpike into a Napoleonic tricorn. "This is either the hottest place in town," he concluded, "or it's really an abandoned gas station."

Venice was about to say "Quo vadis?" but she slapped herself.

"Are we tired?" she asked. "Is it that bad?"

There was a profound pause, the pause that will undoubtedly precede the launch of nuclear warheads.

"Yup," said Guy.

16

Nightcrawlers

At Guy's request, the limousine dropped Guy, Venice and Licky a few blocks from the loft. There was a bakery nearby, and the trio stopped in for fresh eclairs.

They walked home from the bakery. Guy loved this part of the morning, when the world divided into two distinct factions, two sides of the street. Heading toward the major avenues, toward the buses and subways and office buildings, were the people who had retired at a reasonable hour, say, eleven o'clock the night before. These people appeared freshly showered, crisp, intent; they wore suits and clean shirts and carried briefcases and folded newspapers. Aimed in a different direction, toward their homes, was another population. These were the nightcrawlers, the partymongers, the diehards, the people like Guy and Venice and Licky. This was a shambling species, notable for smeary makeup, drooping hems and bleary, heavy-lidded eyes. These were people who had spent the night dancing and dearly needed a rest. Some of these people had caroused in strange beds and had grabbed their clothes and escaped as the sun came up.

In retreat, the nightcrawlers all carried a pastry, or a cup of coffee from a Greek coffee shop. Guy and Venice had their arms around each other, leaning together, as if they were struggling across an inhuman wilderness toward a warm, candlelit encampment. Even Licky sagged. He was barely able to raise his head and search for attractive men. There was a camaraderie to these moments, a fellowship that stretched across the city. The nightcrawlers code was in effect, a code containing a single unbreakable commandment: don't call me before noon—I won't be up.

As Guy neared his home, he identified comrades along the way. She's one, he thought, watching a girl in a trench coat worn over an evening gown, as she sifted her bag for her keys. He's one, the man carrying his shirt, wearing a bomber jacket over his bare flesh, standing on a corner trying to recall which way was west. And look at those two—a man and a woman on roller skates, taking turns pushing each other along. Guy nodded at each of these people and received a nod in reply. These mutual glances held a companionable, unspoken sentiment: "I know what *you've* been doing."

Passing a shop window, Guy caught a glimpse of Venice and himself, in their wilted spangles. Venice had snagged a stocking, and her hair was even more tousled than she ordinarily calculated. Guy had slung his tux jacket over his back, with Sinatra aplomb.

"Look," said Guy, pointing at the reflection, "it's us."

Venice peered at the window.

"Hello, darlings," she said.

"We look nice," said Guy. He scowled at the window, trying to look evil.

Venice studied her husband. She laughed.

"You are the silliest man in New York."

"I am?" asked Guy, surprised.

"Yes," said Venice, kissing him.

"Good," Guy decided. Then they kissed again and walked home.

Guy suspected he should be more gloomy, more angst-ridden, in order to become truly stylish. Many Manhattanites prefer depression and unending introspection, but Guy couldn't indulge. When Guy thought about people starving, or illness, he would feel ashamed for his own good fortune. Guy knew he had little to complain of; any sulking would be almost obscene. People who take taxis should never grumble.

As a rule, New Yorkers have too much time and too much money. They begin to think excessively, mostly about their tiniest problems. With enough nurture, these minor kinks can flourish and require therapy. Only then can the Manhattan neurotic rejoice. While Guy found this phenomenon entertaining, he couldn't get the hang of it. Guy tried to simulate depression. He would attempt the haggard, proudly pinched expression of the analysis junkie. He would try to call his friends' answering services and sob. Ultimately, he would founder; he would neglect to blame everything on his mother, wicked as she was. Guy just wasn't built for anxiety.

After entering the loft, Licky immediately put on the television. He curled up on the floor in front of the set to catch his favorite program, an exercise series called "Morning Midriff." This show featured men in brief apparel writhing to dance music and discussing their hamstrings.

"Look," said Licky. "Nine a.m. and they're still dancing. I worship this show. I hate the idea of everyone conking out at once."

There was nothing Licky didn't like about TV. He basked in the video beam, as if it were a sunlamp. Sometimes Licky suspected that he liked TV more than sex; perhaps this was because he found even bad TV appealing. Before Licky went to sleep, he kissed the TV. Licky felt the TV never got enough physical affection.

Guy and Venice went to the bedroom and shut the door. They dropped their clothes into stylish little drifts on the floor, creating a minefield of rumpled satin and discarded flannel. They proved the depth of their love by appearing before one another with slipshod hair and scrubbed faces. They patted the dog, who was asleep, an open magazine at his side.

It had been a night like so many others, a fun night, the kind that can make you feel two thousand years old. Guy and Venice fell into bed, too beat for sex, cuddling instead, weary bunnies, ragged but safe. They did not worry about the future, as they had every reason to believe Manhattan's nightspots were shuttered for the next few hours.

"You're sleeping with a working man," whispered Guy.

"I am?" said Venice, trying to imagine whom Guy might be referring to. This morning's tycoon? Derek? The building's superintendent?

"Guy!" she whispered, remembering, and very happy.

17

The Morning After

Guy and Venice awoke late the next afternoon, as if they'd spent a long quiet weekend at a country inn. They lazed about for hours, nibbling on each other and taking baths. Licky snored in the next room, the television yammering away like a doting relative. Danilo lay sprawled on his stomach, too sluggish to play with his rubber hydrant or locate a cigarette.

Guy settled on the bed, his hair damp, and watched the naked Venice apply her makeup in the Black Forest mirror. Guy loved this ritual, as Venice became artist and model in one. Guy was fascinated. He followed every stroke as Venice outlined her lips with a camel's hair brush, a brush intended for the movements of fine Swiss watches.

Guy had no wish to change Venice, to organize her life, to insist on domestic compromises. Should Venice change, should she attempt conventional behavior, she would not be Venice. And being Venice took all her concentration. Look at her, Guy thought with endless admiration, she works so hard!

"Venice, are you expecting anyone?" Guy asked, as the scrapings at the front door grew more insistent.

Venice did not answer, embroiled in a crucial lower lash negotiation.

"Licky?" Guy called out, but Licky was asleep, or pharmaceutically unavailable.

The scrapings at the door increased and were accompanied by an accented voice piping, "Beep beep! Beep beep!" in imitation of an automobile horn. Guy decided he had better investigate. He tugged his voluptuous white terry robe shut and pulled on a single black racing glove.

"I'll get it," he told the dog, and he marched out and opened the front door.

"Oh Mister Guy!" cooed Salima. "It is being you!"

"Hi!" said Guy. "How are you?"

"Oh Mister Guy," Salima repeated, "I am finding you!"

"Gee, can I help you?" asked Guy, trying to remember if he had planned a cocktail party or rung for a Fadood. Before he could decide, Salima rushed into the loft and stood in the center of the room, hopping from foot to foot and making small, appreciative chirping noises.

"Oh Mister Guy! The tent of Mister Guy! It is being too much the wonderfulness! No, that is being the old thing to say, it is being . . . it is being . . . funkadelic!"

"Thanks," said Guy. "I'm sorry, it's kind of bare really. I haven't gotten around to finding anything, you know how it is."

"Oh Mister Guy," said Salima, charging toward him. "You are the only one ever! And I am finding you!"

"You are?" said Guy, as Salima backed him toward the Coca-Cola refrigeration unit. "Gee, I don't think I understand . . ."

As Guy leapt on top of the refrigeration unit, hoping to avoid the Arab maiden's imminent attack, he noticed several none-too-subtle changes in Salima's appearance. Her flight from the Club de had resulted in the purchase of several day-glo plastic leis. A pair of bobbing antennae sprouted from Salima's head, mounted on a plastic headband. Salima had also replaced her heirloom nose-ring with a safety pin.

"Wait," said Guy, confused. "Are you really an Arab, or are you from New Jersey?"

"Oh Mister Guyness," Salima twittered, as she climbed up beside her prey and dragged Guy down until they both lay flat atop the refrigeration unit. "You are the cutest pie! You are the only one ever! Before, all are saying, 'Yes, Oded Ben Fadood, of courseness, Oded Ben Fadood, please be taking my she-goat, Oded Ben Fadood!' But last night, you are saying, 'NO, ODED BEN FADOOD!' And he is going into the street, boom boom boom! It is being so much the wonderfulness, it is being . . . too lesbian in the words!"

"Uhm, Mrs. Fadood . . ." Guy began.

"Oh Mister Guy," said Salima, covering Guy's throat with kisses, "you are too much the fabness. You are not understanding. Fadood, the old one he is being, with much the smelliness. A terrible life is mine. I am young girl, in tent with my brothers; all is love. But brothers say, 'Salima, you are beautiful too much; we deserve less. We are dirt of the camel,' brothers say this, 'you are desert blossom.' Fadood is near, they sell me."

"They sell you? Really?" asked Guy, trying to gracefully shy Salima's hand from the belt of his robe.

"Two jackals," said Salima proudly, "because virgin I am! At palace I am put in the oil and the pretty things, so Fadood will have the pleasure. Much pleasure he have. 'Salima,' he say, 'why you do so much pleasure? Hassad, take back one jackal.' With wives and others I am put; at first they are not liking. They take out my hair and use many stones. Then I make Fadood get picture box from America and happiness is everyone."

"Picture box?" asked Guy, "You mean TV? Salima, oh, um, could I have my belt back, okay?"

"The box with the laughing, yes. Why are you wearing all

of this? It is being too much the warm! At first we do not see who is laughing, we think box is perhaps laughing at wives of Fadood. Fadood, he say, 'Wives, you are emptyheads; it is Allah laughing.' This, it is a true part?"

"Uhm . . . yes," said Guy, as he tried to prevent his robe from inching down his shoulders, "it is Allah laughing. Now, Salima, you live in a palace and you have TV—gee, what's the problem?"

"I am telling. I am favorite wife, Fadood says Salima is favorite. This is because I am not with the overbite. Other wives, they are with the overbite, so they are wearing the chador. We are telling American peoples chador is for Allah, but is really for the teeth that are like the bucks. I am bringing many modern things to the wives—the bleaching and the picture box and the dark eyecovers, and Fadood is happiness. Then I am bringing other modern thing to wives, and Fadood is not happiness."

"What?" asked Guy, Salima's lips now dangerously ticklish. "What else did you bring?"

"My brother Arat."

"Oh. So, did the wives like Arat?"

"They are liking him very much. I am saying, 'Fadood, this is being the modern way,' and he is saying, 'Salima, I will take off camel rope and items of restraining in the morning.' He is not understanding; he is being the foreign one, the barbarian—this is right?"

"Salima, come on, please, stop it, I'll get all giggly, couldn't you just sort of sneak around? You know, with Arat?"

"This I am trying, but is difficulty. Other wives they are grabbing, they are saying, 'I have Arat tonight; is being my turn.' I am saying, 'No, sir.' They are telling Fadood, they are saying, 'Salima is like desert blossom, allowing anyone to be smelling her.' I say, 'Your pardon I am begging, Arat is like desert sand, he is getting into everything.' Hassad comes, and he is using the camel rope and the items of restraining on all the wives; there is much trouble. We are coming to America, I am saying, 'Here we will be the modern ones; here Fadood will be learning.' "

"And is he? Being more modern? I'm sure he is, he's a great guy, Salima, please—*Salima! . . .*"

"No! He is being the worseness! He is being the beast with the horn of fire! But you are saying 'NO!' to him. You are saying, 'Fadood, be letting the wives be free!' You are being the sweetness in the smelling, and with no hairiness on the nose! I am looking in the everywhere for you, and the taxi person is saying, 'Oh yes, Mister Guy,' and he is taking me here! It is the will of Allah! You are the baddest of the fucking of the mothers!"

Suddenly, another gauze-clad figure appeared in the doorway. "Salima!" she cried.

"Tira!" said Salima.

"Mister Guy," said Tira, advancing. Tira now sported a blonde afro wig perched atop her veiled head. "Mister Guy, we are finding you!"

"Ladies, *please,* " said Guy, his robe somewhere on the floor. "It's really early, I'm married, I haven't eaten anything . . ."

"Oh, Mister Guy," said Tira, hoisting herself onto the crowded refrigeration unit, "you have the blueness in the hair, and the sweetness in the breath . . ."

"I am seeing him first," sniffed Salima. "Oh Mister Guy, I am looking everywhere for you."

"That's nice, Salima. I mean, I feel really special and all, but—"

"Salima! Tira!"

"Latinda!"

"Latinda, be coming over here, and be seeing Mister Guy, who is saving us from Fadood."

"Oh, Mister Guy," said Latinda, kissing Guy's toes and flinging her frisbee into a far corner, "you are having such prettiness toes . . ."

"Oh Mister Guy," said Salima, "you are being prettiness everywhere . . ."

"Salima! Tira! Latinda!"

"Ramira!"

"Hofstra!"

"Cardima!"

"Now, girls," Guy sputtered, as his naked body was enveloped in a caravan of fine brown flesh. "Girls, ladies . . . oh my God . . ."

"Oh, Mister Guy," said Hofstra, above the wet, purring din, "do not be with the worrying! Fadood is always having the happiness with the many wives. He is saying the American words when it is being desired. Latinda, what is Fadood saying when all wives are to be coming as one wife to bring the happiness?"

"He is saying," said Latinda, " 'Soup's on!' "

"Thank you, Latinda," Guy managed to moan, feeling like a football buried deep in a scrimmage, desired yet battered.

"And Ramira," said Ramira.

"Yes, right, thank you, Ramira," Guy moaned.

"And Salima."

"And Salima . . ."

"And Tira."

"And Tira . . ."

"And Hofstra."

"And Hofstra . . ."

"And Hassad."

"And Hassad?"

"Hassad!"

"AIIIIIIIIIIEEEEEEEEE!!!!!"

With the untimely appearance of Fadood's henchman, the room convulsed in a riot of whirling gauze and Coptic epithets. The wives leaped from the refrigerator, hurling small objects and pocketing others in their flight from certain punishment. Within seconds Guy was left alone and naked on the floor. He sat surrounded by six pairs of sunglasses and a T-shirt that read, "My Mommy Went to New York and All I Got Was This Lousy T-Shirt." Guy also had a grape popsicle stuck to his forehead.

"Gee, you must be Hassad," Guy said to the only remaining Arab in the room. "Boy, I'm really sorry about all this . . ."

"Again you are being the one," said Hassad. "You are the one from the Club of de. I am to be telling Fadood."

"But . . . but . . ." said Guy.

"I am to be telling Fadood."

Hassad shot his cuffs and spat on his own sleeve, a gesture of the utmost derision among his people. The saliva dripping from his slim Italian sports jacket, Hassad laughed cruelly and left.

"Darling," said Licky, rousing himself from the corner where he had been dozing on a pile of opera gloves, "was there someone at the door?"

"Yes," said Guy, decisively.

"Guy," said Venice, coming to the bedroom door, sensual now that her lips were done. "Guy, why did you leave? I'm lonely . . ."

"I'm sorry," said Guy, always helpless where Venice's lips were concerned, "I was getting the door."

"Was it anyone?" asked Venice. "Was it for me?"

"No," said Guy, trying to forget the whole incident. "Have you, um, seen the belt to my robe?"

"Here it is," said Venice, picking up the belt and trailing

it behind her as she returned to the bedroom. "I'm going to eat it."

Licky went back to sleep, while Guy and Venice romped in the bedroom as husband and wife. Everyone was so busy that the dog had to answer the door the next time and greet the police.

18

The Trial: The Prosecution

The police arrived late in the afternoon and informed Guy he was under arrest. Oded Ben Fadood had pressed charges, managing to have Guy held responsible for assault, the kidnapping of the Fadood women, abusive language and "interfering with territorial waters." The summons came from the city courts, at the instructions of the United Nations and OPEC, the international oil cartel.

The police officers waited patiently while Guy got dressed. A sergeant was particularly helpful in locating Venice's white cashmere top. Venice was so grateful that she shared a joint with the sergeant, so they could both feel more pulled together.

Guy was escorted to a police station and booked. Venice and Licky also insisted on being fingerprinted, initiating a brief vogue for blackened fingertips among the cognoscenti. Licky adored the police station and had to be coaxed into leaving. "Look at all this," Licky had moaned. "Criminals, and thugs, and roughnecks—it's an *oasis.*"

Bail was quickly raised. Venice called on certain gentlemen for substantial sums: "Darling, it's an investment," she told Mr. Carlingcurl. The remaining funds were poached from a charity blowout for the Homeless. "The Homeless?" Licky said. *"Please.* What about the truly needy, the people without second homes? Where's *my* place at the beach?"

The accused and his party returned home after midnight, bone-tired. Guy and Venice fell into bed and tried to make sense of the day's events.

"Guy," said Venice, "is this big trouble? Will I need new clothes?"

"Boy, I don't know," said Guy, "I think it's all a misunderstanding. I mean I have a lawyer and everything, I don't think I did anything wrong, but it's kind of hard to say."

"It is," Venice agreed. "If you'd killed somebody, there'd be a body and blood, then we wouldn't have any problems. It'd be fabulous. But this is too *fromage.* I know, we'll just have them for dinner and explain—the Fadoods, I mean. That's it."

"Gee, it would be great, but I don't think we can," said Guy. "There are thousands of them. We don't have enough chairs."

"It's really kind of a hoot," said Venice, emphasizing the positive side of things. "It's not like there's *anything* coming up. Look, Danilo brought his toy in, he wants to help. It'll be the best, Licky already knows what he's wearing."

"What he's wearing?" asked Guy. "Where?"

"On the stand," said Venice.

"Oh boy," said Guy.

Guy was granted a speedy trial, as Jon Gelle was interested in possible film rights. Tanzo Matta designed a lavish trial wardrobe for Venice, and the sketches were leaked to *Glaze.* There was ample press coverage in the dailies as well. The headlines included "ARABIAN NIGHTMARES," "BOILING OIL!" and, in the more proletarian paper, "GUY—HERO OR SLASHER?"

Guy's lawyers recommended that he maintain a low profile and consider undergoing a religious rebirth. It was suggested that the addition of a child might create a more sympathetic image for the Hubers, but Licky's purchase of one led only to the most regrettable publicity.

A jury was selected, and things got under way with the Honorable Nadine LaTarga presiding. Judge LaTarga was a full-figured black woman of unimpeachable standing and much good humor. She had attended the nation's finest law schools, where she had gained a reputation for diligence, precision and wearing slippers to class. Judge LaTarga was now the top-ranking circuit official in New York State, and the governorship was rumored. People responded to Judge LaTarga, sensing an innate fairness to her decisions, an unshakable integrity. In her robes, Judge LaTarga much resembled a first alto in an inner-city Baptist choir.

Guy was awed by Judge LaTarga. He was almost glad he had been arrested, just so he could watch her in action. If Judge LaTarga said he was guilty, Guy knew he would be. He admired her command of the courtroom, her comprehensive knowledge of local and federal statutes, and her tendency to eat during the various attorneys' presentations.

The early days of the trial proved uneventful. The case against Guy was presented by the prosecution. Oded Ben Fadood's lawyers indicated Guy's many felonies. Guy, it was alleged, had charged at Fadood with a bolo and mace and had then fired three pistol shots directly into Fadood's head.

Witnesses testified that Guy had abducted the many Mrs. Fadoods at dagger-point. Guy had then forced the Fadood women to commit heinous acts. These acts included blasphemy, adultery and the use of a striped toothpaste.

Fadood took the stand. On his counsel's advice, he wore a necktie and a pocket handkerchief pinned to his burnoose. Fadood began his testimony with a display of much naive fervor, his palms clutching his breast, a gesture of innocent emotion familiar to any culture based in haggling.

"I am coming to the America," Fadood began, "where all are having the fun, where all are being the equal ones, where all are allowed the many happy things."

"Cut the bull, floppy," said Judge LaTarga. "I don't wanna hear it. All that equal stuff—you know why they come up with that? To trick the colored folks into singin' opera. Honey, that old-time slaveman, maybe he whup us, maybe he take our children, maybe we pick till we die, but at least he never make us sing that fuckin' Puccini-weenie."

"Objection!" said the prosecuting attorney.

"Leave me alone," said Judge LaTarga, slinging a French fry at the prosecuting attorney. She turned back to Fadood and sighed heavily. "Get on wit' your business."

"It is so much the terrible, all of the horribles that are being done to Fadood," said Fadood, weeping. "I am going to have the fun in the place of fun, the Club of de, and then, boom boom boom, there is the hitting much about my head and the encountered on my person! My blood is being on the street and my arms are falling off and my brains are rolling out of my head under the car! And he, the most evil one, the one by the doorway, he is saying, 'Fadood, he is dead! Now I can be taking his wives!'"

Fadood paused, fell to his knees and keened. Judge LaTarga opened a beer, shaking it first so that the spray drenched Fadood.

"Whoops!" said Judge LaTarga, "Ain't I a mad thing? You was sayin'?"

"He is taking my wives!" Fadood screeched, wiping his face and climbing back onto the stand. "He is taking them to the bad place, they are screaming, 'No! no! no! We are for Fadood!' But he is with the forcing of his lips! He is with the forcing and the magazines and the filthiness I cannot be imagining as I am the servant of Allah and the honorary doctor from the University of Southern California! Wives, when they are being rescued, they are with the water from the eyes, they are saying, 'Now we are unfit for the pleasure of Fadood, now we are being the entrails of the baboon!' They are begging Fadood, 'Please be using the camel rope and the items of restraining and be putting our hands in the blender!' I am coming to the America and now I am blind and crippled and with no wives and I am never with the dancing!"

Here Fadood, overcome, grabbed Judge LaTarga's cheese taco and took a sizable bite. The Judge slammed her gavel onto Fadood's hand and he dropped the taco.

"I am the saddest of all men," groaned Fadood, sucking his hand. "I am not even with the dating! It is all being the fault of him! Of the rutting hyena with the snout of drooling! Of the one at the doorway!"

"Honey, could you kinda indicate that one?" requested Judge LaTarga.

"It is being like the mark upon my head and the dull knife in my parts! I am remembering the face in the always, until I am with the dying in the arms of my beloved mother, the only woman of cleanliness, Betty Ben Fadood!" said Fadood. "It is being THAT ONE!" Fadood thundered, and in a sweeping gesture pointed to Licky.

"Darling," said Licky. "I mean, really."

"You may step down," said Judge LaTarga. "Whoa! Ain't he somethin'!"

19

The Trial: The Defense

After a week's testimony, the prosecution rested. The trial had remained newsworthy, and Guy spent the weekend judging a beauty pageant in Fort Lauderdale. Venice was photographed smiling bravely at a variety of First Nights and serious French restaurants. Licky decided to auction his memoirs and began interviewing ghostwriters; the book's working title was *The Huber Case: Licky Banes's Backstairs Diary.*

Guy's defense began with a well-researched look at the facts of the case. Guy's lawyers indicated the mistaken identities involved and offered documented proof that Renzo and Carmine had been physically responsible for the expulsion of Fadood from the Club de. Guy's lawyers wanted to subpoena Bruce, Debbie and Michelle, but no one would go to New Jersey to serve them.

Fadood's harem could not be called to the stand, as wives are not permitted to testify against their husband. The women could not even be located for depositions, as Fadood had felt their privacy was best assured in a sealed suite in a hotel where requests for barbed wire went unquestioned. Guy's legal team was, however, able to enter into evidence the hideous plastic corsages, Whitman's Samplers and birthstone tietacks Guy had been receiving. These gifts were always accompanied by garish confirmation cards reading "Allah Be Praised," followed by six gooey lipstick X's.

Guy's case was on the upswing, with the jurors nodding sympathetically, until the third week of the trial, when Guy's character witnesses were asked to take the stand.

Guy's mother appeared first, as Guy's lawyers felt it would be awfully nice. Mrs. Huber was sworn in and was asked to attest to her son's honesty, judgment and overall strength of character.

"Guy? My youngest?" Mrs. Huber began. "Why, I think he's terrific. I don't know what that is in his hair, but I'm sure it will grow out, at least it isn't in his eyes, like Sniggy Derryman's boy, I always say he looks like a sheepdog. Do you know Sniggy? She's a great gal, she and Tarp have such a pretty place on the Cape, they go clamming not ten feet from their front door. I've always liked Sniggy, she makes the most delicious rum nog, we always drop by over the holidays, she uses cloves, that's the secret, and vermouth. I understand she's getting her license back just next month, isn't that grand?"

Mrs. Huber paused for breath, and handed Judge LaTarga a shopping bag full of neatly folded, fraying blouses and laundered dustrags. On top of these castoffs rested an envelope containing a generous Easter bonus.

"We're so proud of our Guy," Mrs. Huber continued, "especially with so many young people turning out poorly, why it's in the paper every day. They're at those nightclubs, putting

Lord knows what in their ears, such a shame, I blame the parents."

"Bye, honey," said Judge LaTarga as Mrs. Huber stepped down.

"Goodbye, dear," Mrs. Huber replied, "the veal was perfect."

Guy's father was not called, but he did send along a note to Guy's dean, promising that Guy would try and apply himself next semester.

Ratallia Parv took the stand next. "Guy, he is gudt," Ratallia told Judge LaTarga. "He is not gudt like negro, chu are negro, chu unnerstand. I am vuman, budt I am also childt. Ve must stop de nuclear madnuss."

Caronia Desti followed Ratallia. "Guy! Guy Huber!" she declaimed. "The *innocence* of guilt!"

Lucy Yates Membrane followed Caronia. She took the stand clutching a raffia tote acquired on a recent DAR package tour of the Yucatan.

"Okay, big gal, whatchoo got to say?" said Judge LaTarga.

Before speaking, Lucy arranged her colorful dirndl, which featured a hand-painted Guadalajara village with cactus, slumbering señor and mission bell. Lucy tugged her Taxco peasant blouse back onto her shoulders (her bust as yet insufficient for the Saucy Rosita effect intended).

"Well, Your Honor," Lucy began, "I've known Guy for ages, and he's always been a gentleman. I collect frogs—my pin is papier-mâché, from Xocoxomillio, which means 'Our Lady Of Crafts,' the work is just lovely. Now, Guy has complimented me on such pieces time and again. I think that tells you something about a person."

"Awright," said Judge LaTarga, who was studying Lucy's sturdy walking brogues.

"Actually, Guy and I grew up together," Lucy continued. "Our families are very close. Aren't the Hubers splendid? My mother, in fact, once remarked, 'That Guy Huber, why can't you be more like him and stop doing that with your ankles.' And I said, *'Mother'* . . . well, actually, it all became very unpleasant."

"Where you get them shoes, honey?" asked Judge LaTarga, "I can never find me a triple E."

"I have them made," said Lucy. Lucy took a moment to re-pin the lush crepe poppy which sat dead center on her head, between the coiled braids. "The nicest man on the Bowery does all my shoes; he's so understanding. Now, when I heard that Guy was in some sort of trouble, I thought, I must do something. Your Honor, I'm sure there's been a dreadful mistake, I just know it. Call it—call it woman's intuition."

"Objection!" shouted the prosecuting attorney.

"On what grounds?" demanded Judge LaTarga, but Lucy had already fled the stand, castanets rattling, in tears of bitter offense.

Guy's legal team saved Venice and Licky for last, feeling that as Guy's closest associates, their testimony would bear the highest moral consequence with the jury.

Licky took the stand wearing an unconstructed, nubby silk suit with the collar turned up, an emerald lapel pin in the shape of a swaying palm, alligator loafers and no socks. His hair was slicked back in a tight twist. He sported clear nail polish, a pince-nez, and carried a gold-tipped ebony walking stick. This was Licky's approximation of responsible male attire, although Marlene Dietrich in a debonair mood was more the image that came to mind.

"Do you swear to tell the truth, the whole truth and nothing but the truth?" asked the baliff.

"Always," said Licky.

There was an outbreak of snickering in the courtroom.

"Ignore them," Licky told the bailiff. "They're nobody."

"State your name."

"Licky Banes. *Yes.*"

"Occupation?"

"Witness."

"Before that."

"Oh. Domestic employee. Oh, and I sometimes do art criticism for the better small magazines. But only seventeenth-century, everything else is really too *triste,* don't you think?"

"How long have you known the accused, and in what capacity?" Guy's attorney asked.

"Guy? La Guy? I've known him forever; who hasn't? Now, what was the rest of the question—my capacity? Too easy, darling, I'll resist. I'm his maid."

"You his what?" said Judge LaTarga.

"His maid. It's backbreaking, but the Hubers are very generous."

"You live-in?" asked Judge LaTarga.

"Oh, yes," said Licky.

"TV?"

"Of course."

"Evenin's free, Tuesdays off?" Judge LaTarga inquired ruthlessly.

"Half-day Tuesday," Licky confessed.

"Young man," said Judge LaTarga to Guy. "Now you in trouble."

"I told you," said Licky, also to Guy. "Oh, but Judge, don't hold it against him. There's always a nice lunch, and he did promise to buy me a chaise. He's heaven, really. For Whitey."

"We'll see," said Judge LaTarga. "So chile, were you there at the time? of the incidents in question?"

"Was I?" said Licky, mortally cut. "Of course, what do you think I do—sit at home, marinating? Honey, I was out that night, it was eternal. And that Fadood person, I mean, if you ask me, he had it coming. I mean, unbleached muslin? And those wives, always in that black, sure it's safe, I suppose it always works. Tomorrow we'll all be wearing it, but, really, I'm tired of it. If you ask me, the entire Arab Republic is nothing but yardage. Now your look," he continued, noting the Judge's robes, "has line, it speaks to me, it says tradition, yes, but with a sense of humor. And the beads are inspired."

"You really think so?" said Judge LaTarga, fingering the brightly painted shards strung on a cord around her neck, the gift of a pre-school grandchild.

"But yes," said Licky. "What are they—Milan? You must've spent a fortune, but, you see, it's worth it. If you showed up at de tonight, you know you'd get in."

"Really?" said Judge LaTarga, astounded.

"Darling, of course," Licky replied. "You're fabulous. I could have you for lunch. I could nibble you till you scream. You are beyond faboo, you are fabtastic. Fab-o-rama. Fabulant."

"Objection, Your Honor!" called one of Fadood's lawyers. "The witness is attempting to influence the bench."

"I beg your *pardon,*" said Licky, pronouncing "pardon" as if it were French.

"Objection overruled," said Judge LaTarga. "Go on, Gigi."

"Well, anywho, Guy is just *quel* swell, I mean, let's face it. No wonder those wives went hog-wild for him; he's just a bug's ear, an absolute devil dog *delish.* I mean, kiss that boy, hug that boy, let him stay up late. As I'm sure you know," Licky continued, leaning toward the judge in his most confidential manner, "everyone in New York is gay, except Guy. He's the control."

"No further questions," said Fadood's lawyer.

"Honey, you can step down now," said Judge LaTarga.

"We'll talk later," said Licky.

"How's Wednesday?" suggested Judge LaTarga.

"I can break it," Licky decided. "Don't you hate sex?"

"Call me, sugar."

"Kisses to you."

Licky stepped down, freezing for a moment and adjusting his profile for the photographers. Returning to his seat in the courtroom, Licky paused as he passed the jury. He stared long and hard at the jurors, perplexed. He didn't know anyone. Licky made a sharp clicking noise with his tongue.

"Who *are* you?" Licky disdainfully asked the jury.

"Do you swear to tell the truth, the whole truth and nothing but the truth?"

Venice, having deposited herself on the stand, continued to nod her head from side to side, rhythmically.

"Do you swear to tell the truth, the whole truth and nothing but the truth?" the bailiff repeated, exasperated.

Venice raised her palm, her eyes closed, and mouthed, "In a minute, darling."

"Your Honor . . ." whined the bailiff.

"Just wait, chile," cautioned Judge LaTarga, "keep your face on."

"All right," said Venice. She removed her headset, shut off the Walkman and shook out her hair. *"Fabulous* song. The best."

Venice grabbed the bailiff's tie and pulled him toward her. She leaned forward and used the reflection from the bailiff's eyeglasses to check her lips.

"Ready, darling," Venice said. "Where's that Bible?"

"Do you swear to tell the truth, the whole truth and nothing but the truth?" the bailiff repeated through clenched teeth.

"Darling, he's my husband."

"State your name."

"Venice Huber."

"Occupation?"

"Well, it's hard to say. I don't model, land of the seventeen bimbos. I don't act—after all, isn't an actress just a model who won't shut up? Let's say, oh—homemaker. Could you die?"

At this point Venice crossed her legs. She was wearing one of Tanzo's finest creations, a leather miniskirt, laced up both sides, with a matching leather bra. The flashbulbs subsided, and Venice opened her bag and took out a cigarette. Fadood, his attorneys, the bailiff and the court stenographer all rushed forward with matches and lighters.

"Mmmmm," said Venice. "You boys."

She accepted a light from the prosecuting attorney, as well as his Dunhill lighter. She took a slow drag on the cigarette and blew the smoke into Fadood's face.

"Where were we?" she asked.

"Were you present on the evening in question?" asked Guy's attorney.

"At de?" Venice tried to remember. "I think so. The black satin strapless! That's right. You'd love it—you animal."

"Would you please tell the court exactly what transpired, as you recall it?"

"Well," said Venice, "it was fabulous. All right, it got boring, but, darling, what doesn't? I hadn't seen Guy for ages, so that was nice. Oh, it's all just dish, you don't want to hear about this." She laughed knowingly. "Do you?"

"Honey," said Judge LaTarga, "what the man means is, did you see that Fadood dude? That night?"

"Now, I don't know," said Venice. "Was it Fadood, was it Jersey, was it the acid? Who can live nowadays? Did you ever just get your hair cut? It wasn't even twenty-four hours. Hair shock. But Guy didn't do anything. Guy is the best. I mean,

I married Guy. And he wouldn't hit anybody—it's too trendy.
All right, we tried it once, but we kept giggling. Renzo and Carmine hit people, they're fabulous. But Guy is sweet. I mean,
we have a *dog*."

"Mrs. Huber," asked Guy's attorney, "to the best of your
knowledge, did Mr. Huber abduct the women of Mr. Fadood's
household?"

Venice froze, in the middle of another drag on her cigarette.

"What do you mean by abduct?" she asked, suspiciously.
"Dinner?"

"We are speaking of kidnapping," the attorney replied,
"which is a federal offense of extreme gravity."

"Kidnapping?" Venice repeated. "Six women? Guy doesn't
even get up until three. And besides, if he did something with
those women, he would never tell me."

"Out of concern for your feelings?" the attorney asked, sympathetically.

Venice stubbed out her cigarette, calmly. She looked up.

"Because I'd rip his face off," she replied.

"Honey, I understand," said Judge LaTarga, nodding. "I am
one thousand percent behind you, damn right. But now, you
think about it. I know you love yo' man, we all love our man,
but he ever get, you know, itchy? Maybe a little wine, hangin'
out with some wrong dudes, messin' where he shouldn't?"

"Is that what your guy does?" asked Venice.

"Honey, don't ask," said Judge LaTarga.

"Men. Too much," said Venice.

"You speak the truth," said Judge LaTarga, as both women
shook their heads ruefully.

"Tell me about it," said Venice. "You know, when they just
sit there, like old farts, 'Honey, I'm tired,' and they won't
dance?"

"Girl, I hear ya," said Judge LaTarga.

"Of course, sometimes it's nice when a guy doesn't like to

dance," Venice considered. "Maybe God invented gay guys to dance, so the other ones could rest. And sometimes it is just too sweet, when they turn into their fathers and you cream, you just *cream.* "

Venice inhaled sharply and ran her hand over her bare throat, moaning slightly.

"Ohhhhhh," said everyone in the courtroom, shifting in their seats and feeling flushed.

"I *know,* " moaned Judge LaTarga, "Lord, they do get to ya."

"They *do,* " whimpered the courtroom.

"Like when they bring you a present," Venice offered, "or when they get all dressed up, and you die, you just die. It's so mean."

"So mean," the courtroom echoed.

"My man, Dolby," Judge LaTarga testified, "he puts on his fine blue suit, with a carnation, and that big ol' diamond pin— honey, you can carry me out in a pine box. Like we be fightin' and cursin' each other, raisin' the dead, an' he just shows up all decked out and how-you-do, with that flower. I just say, 'Dolby, I'm gonna smack you one.' "

"Lock 'em up!" Venice concluded. "It's the answer. Too much."

"DO IT!" cried the courtroom.

"I wish I could," agreed the judge. "Fine blue suit in the first degree. Twenty to life."

"THE CHAIR!" said the courtroom.

"I love it," said Venice.

"Honey," said Judge LaTarga. "Venice—that your name, right? It's pretty. I got me a sister, Teflon, I gotta tell her. Now Venice, sweet thing—your man, he be guilty?"

"Oh no," said Venice firmly, "he be fabulous."

"Girl," declared Judge LaTarga, "you may step down."

The courtroom burst into applause.

Venice stood up. She paused. Then she bent down to straighten the nonexistent seam of one of her stockings.

Pandemonium ensued. Judge LaTarga banged her gavel to quiet the room. "Leave the girl be!" she commanded.

Venice stepped off the stand and walked across the courtroom. She glanced at the jury, and every juror felt a split-second of libidinous eye contact. "I love you," Venice mouthed.

Finally Venice reached her seat, directly behind Guy. She gave him a ferocious hug and bit his ear. Then she sat down.

"Darlings," Venice asked, anxious about her testimony, "was I all right?"

"Brava!" said Licky, almost speechless. "Costa del Brava!"

"You were great!" said Guy. "You were the best one!"

"Please," said Licky, "Best Supporting in a Musical."

"Enchanting!" cried Caronia from across the room, standing on a bench and continuing the ovation. "Yumsy!"

"I love the Judge," said Venice. "Isn't she the best?"

"Darling, she's *yours,*" said Licky.

At that point the bailiff issued a final warning, calling for silence or he would clear the courtroom.

"Oh please," Venice whispered, "don't you just hate that?"

Guy was scheduled to take the stand on the final day of the trial, but he overslept.

"I'm such a jerk," he said, when Venice returned to the loft and told him the proceedings had wound up. "Boy, should I get a note or something?"

"Don't worry," said Venice. "I told them you were out late. I'm sure they'll understand. I mean, of *course.*"

20

The Jury

Guy was convicted after an extremely brief deliberation by the jurors, who considered matters over salads and a light California chablis. The jurors, a bold cross-section of American life, sat around a solid oak table in a paneled chamber, fondling their meal.

"I just don't like the sound of it," said Leona Scribette, a retired registered nurse from Bayside, "and so soon after the holidays. This is delicious."

"Why was that one chick so big," asked Manny Gargo, eager to return to his floor duties at the 89¢ Store ("Any Item Only 89¢"), "and his mom, how come she talks like that? Don't it hurt?"

"His wife was somethin'," said Regal Hawkins, whose three wives thought he was dead. "How many bottles we got?"

"If you like that sort of thing," said Jennifer Rittle, fingering her many chains and shoving a shoulderpad back into place. "I'm the Tab."

"And why is that man their maid?" asked Mrs. Scribette incisively. "Are these walnuts?"

No one was able to answer Mrs. Scribette's questions with authority. This did not augur well, as suspicion breeds suspicion.

"It's a disgrace," said Curmloin Tunne, purveyor of rare books. "That Mr. Fadood came all the way across the Atlantic Ocean, and look what he saw. A lazybones with a sissy maid and a wife who . . . well, she looked right at me with only one thing on her mind."

"Hey, what you talkin', she was lookin' at *me* with only one thing on her mind," protested Mr. Hawkins.

"Oh, I thought . . ." said Mrs. Scribette, who turned a graphic scarlet and was unable to continue.

"I think it's disgusting," declared Mr. Tunne. "The dressing is rancid. If he were my son, I'd be ashamed."

"I've never been to the Club de," said Miss Rittle, "and I don't want to go. Oh no, I couldn't—well, just a nibble. If you're sure you don't want it."

"He shoulda pleaded insanity," said Mr. Gargo. "You Jewish?"

"It's a terrible crime," said Lenka Tenty, who, before release, had been designated "harmless" by the psychologists at the State Farm.

"That boy must think we're idiots," said Mr. Tunne, in the piercing tones that caused youngsters to steal his bicycle.

"These *are* walnuts," said Mrs. Scribette, and that settled it.

Judge LaTarga was quite upset by the verdict, shaking her head and shooting Mr. Hawkins a particularly sharp glance. "I'm real sorry," she said to Guy as he stood before the bench. "They must be high."

Guy was shaken by his conviction, but he remembered his manners, his P's and Q's, the blessing of a decent upbringing, and he told the judge, "It's okay. Really."

"You CREEPS," said Venice, hurling her shoe, bag and Walkman at the jury. "You SLIME!"

"I mean, really," said Licky. "Trial by jury. It's barbaric."

Sentence would not be passed until the following morning, and Guy was allowed out on bail prior to the hearing. He, Venice and Licky repaired to the Utopia Diner for sundaes and strategy.

"So what can they do," said Licky, "put you in prison?"

"Really?" asked Venice. "Prison? That's so mean! What is their problem?"

"Imagine," said Licky. "Thousands of lonely men, crammed into inadequate housing, sex-starved and predatory. Oh, I'm sorry—that's the Village. Prison is probably awful."

Guy was unable to process his conviction or to make any sense of the past few weeks of his life. He felt helpless, borne along on a rushing river of lunacy. Guy was too polite to question his fate. He assumed that God knew what He was doing and that God would protect him. Guy imagined God to be a sort of omniscient Jamaican housekeeper, or a bountiful grandparent, shooing away evil and providing treats. Guy did not believe in a vengeful God. He believed in the Easter Bunny and the Tooth Fairy and all the other generous modern deities.

"Gee, I don't know what to do," said Guy. "I guess I'm guilty, so I guess I should be punished, but it's all so weird. But thanks, you guys, for everything. You were terrific. And the trial was sort of neat. Boy, see what happens when you get a job?"

21

The Sentencing

Realizing that they would have to appear in court at 9 a.m., Guy and his crew decided not to go to sleep at all. They spent the night before the sentencing in their typical manner, trying not to dwell on whatever misfortune the upcoming hearing might hold.

At eight o'clock the next morning, everyone swallowed any residue deemed inappropriate for a courthouse appearance, and headed downtown.

"We know we'll get in," Licky said.

Guy and his cohorts, disheveled and barely focusing, filed into the courtroom and stood before Judge LaTarga.

"Hi, darling," said Venice.

"Hi, honey," said the judge. "Ain't you a sight."

"Not so loud," said Licky, massaging his pounding temples, "I'll lose the baby."

"Hi, Judge," said Guy. "I'm back."

"I know it, chile," said Judge LaTarga, "ain't it a shame?"

"Yes," said Guy, trying not to nod. "Gee, do you have any lime juice?"

"Oh, honey, no," said Judge LaTarga, "take a little bitty beer and a raw egg, you be fine."

"Where's the ladies'?" asked Venice, clutching her mouth.

"Oh, *Nadine,*" Licky groaned.

The bailiff called things to order, and the particulars of Guy's conviction were repeated. As Judge LaTarga was about to pass sentence, there was a commotion at the rear of the courtroom. The hubbub mounted, and then, with a startling velocity, a familiar gauze-clad figure pitched herself before the bench. The woman dragged a length of heavy chain along behind her, soldered to an iron cuff about her ankle, and her chador was in tatters.

"Please, please, you must be with the listening!" the woman sobbed. "I am Salima!"

"You who?" said Judge LaTarga.

"I am being the wife of Fadood, from where all is the terrible! And I am being for Guy, of the little feet!"

"Darling?" said Venice to her husband.

"She's no one," said Guy, looking away. "From school."

"Now, honey, what can we do for ya?" Judge LaTarga asked Salima.

"Oh, black one of the judgment, you are doing much the wrongness! The Guy one, he is not of the guilty things!"

"Huh?" said Judge LaTarga.

"I am with the escaping from Fadood, and I am coming to the Guy, who I am loving as the only!"

"*What,* darling?" said Venice, trying to remain composed.

"Hassad is watching the picture box, in the hotel," Salima confided, "and I am escaping! Hassad is watching the woman of the red hair, the Lucy one with Ethel, and he is going 'Ha, ha, ha!' And I am escaping for the Guy, so now I am going 'Ha, ha, ha!' "

"Ha. Ha. Ha," said Venice, rather distinctly.

"Oh yes, the Guy is with the dreaminess in the loving, and not with the smelling of the breath and the hairiness in the nose and the camel rope! The wives of Fadood, we must be with the speaking out—we are not being the wives of Fadood, we are wives of the Guy!"

With that, Salima knelt before Guy, her head bowed. The other wives filed into the courtroom with a certain awkwardness, as they remained shackled at the ankle to one another. On a count from Salima, the wives lurched to their knees and arrayed themselves prettily and noisily at Guy's feet.

"I am for the Guy," said Latinda, reverently.

"I am the Mrs. Guy," said Cardima, her eyes misting.

"I am the chattel and goat of the Guy," said Hofstra, licking Guy's calf.

"I am forever of the Guy," said Ramira.

"I am with always Mister Guy," said Tira.

"The wives of Guy," declared Salima proudly. "This we are being."

There was a hush in the courtroom as the spectators took in the tableau and Guy tried to delicately remove Hofstra from his leg.

"Do you know these women?" Venice asked Guy, after a pause.

" 'Cause honey, if what they say be true," said Judge La-Targa, "maybe we have us a whole 'nother look at things. Is they yo' wives?"

"Guy?" asked Venice, almost in tears, with a half-note of rage.

"*Guy,*" said Licky, impressed. "Not *bad.*"

"Chile?" inquired Judge LaTarga.

Guy looked at the Arab women gathered beneath him. They were adoring, radically submissive, willing to perform any task, endure any humiliation, and fully able to snatch him from prison's terror.

Then Guy looked at Venice. She was stunning, promiscuous, fatally jealous and increasingly livid. And crying. Guy had never seen Venice's mascara run.

"Your Honor," said Guy.

"Nadine," said Judge LaTarga, kindly.

"Nadine," said Guy, standing very straight. "This is so weird. I never saw these women before in my whole life."

22

Up the River

Guy was sentenced to many months in prison, and Judge La-Targa wished him well. Then Guy was shackled and handcuffed and hauled out of the courtroom by a pair of beefy, sneering police matrons. Guy was allowed no time to bid Venice farewell, nor to acknowledge the inconsolable Fadood wives.

Guy was hustled into a heavily armored van. The engine rumbled, and Guy struggled to his knees, peeking out the small grilled window at the rear of the vehicle. When the van stopped at a light, Guy noticed a newsstand on a corner. Tabloids covered the stand, all featuring photos of Venice entering the courtroom or on the stand or getting out of a taxi. These photos were captioned "Darling!" and "Mrs. Huber Testifies" and "Justice in Heels."

A bit further on, Guy caught sight of Venice's celestial blue eyes on a billboard, tossing Times Square a come-hither glance. As a result of the trial, Venice had been approached for many endorsements; the billboard promoted her favorite perfume, a scent entitled "Guilty."

The last Guy saw of Venice was her weeping face projected on fifty TV screens in the window of an appliance outlet. Venice was being interviewed outside the courtroom. Through her tears, she managed to gaze directly into the camera and blow a kiss.

Guy found this series of farewells quite touching; it was as if Venice had run along behind the van, popping up everywhere. Boy, what a wonderful city, Guy thought, as he watched Manhattan melt into the distance.

The trip to the Men's Correctional Facility at Albany took over four hours, and Guy was allowed no food or drink. Luckily, the armored van held laundry, so Guy was more than comfortable, and the driver was able to find a soul station broadcasting out of Westchester.

The van arrived at the Men's Facility at dusk. Guy squinted through the grilled window. He was able to make out a long, low building surrounded by smaller structures. A jagged tower loomed in the distance, and Guy thought he could discern a gallows. Everything was surrounded by high mesh fences crowned with broken glass. Dogs could be heard howling, followed by the even more soul-shattering sound of dogs who have suddenly stopped howling.

A uniformed figure with a weapon slung over his shoulder strode out to greet the van, check for contraband and allow entry. Guy hoped he might be mistaken for laundry, but this was not the case. The guard glanced into the back of the van and nodded. The truck rolled forward into the compound.

A searchlight swept the grounds as Guy was dragged across the yard and into the main building. He was ushered into a small, concrete room, where his shackles and handcuffs were removed. Medical and psychiatric exams were administered.

Guy was found to be free of head lice, hernias and violent tendencies. The prison psychologist, studying Guy's Rorschach results, assured Guy that sexual fantasies involving Venice Huber were more than common.

Guy was brought to a supply room and handed a shabby, anonymous gray cotton uniform and hobnailed work boots with steel toes. The look was strikingly similar to an outfit Guy had worn all through college, except it was clean. Guy was jammed onto a tin stool, where he received a short haircut, which obliterated his blue streak. Guy stared at the floor as the neon strands fell like slashes of graffiti. My hair, Guy thought, my blue hair! Guy became almost a child, he grew frightened, as if the trim were physically painful.

After his haircut, Guy was handed a toothbrush and a Bible. Guy had never read the Bible and wondered if he had time for a quick skim before greeting his fellow inmates. He opened the book and immediately recalled the justification for his lifetime resistance to Christianity: terribly small type. Before Guy could reconsider this position, he was ordered to report to Cellblock 18, at once, for cell assignment.

Guy was led down a labyrinth of dark corridors by a hunched orderly. Their footsteps echoed melodramatically. Iron doors and gates slammed shut as they passed through, resounding with all the heightened finality one could desire. They approached a tiered cellblock, chillingly silent and lit only by exposed bulbs casting ominous, *film noir*-ish shadows.

The orderly opened a last gate with a skeleton key from his clattering hoop and cautioned Guy to wait until the block captain appeared. Then, with a demonic chuckle, the orderly disappeared. Guy was unutterably alone, shorn and anxious, deep in the ulcerated belly of the American penal system.

After a mildewed eon, there was a sharp sound from the far end of the cellblock. Guy detected a hulking figure moving deliberately toward him. The figure's tread was lumbering and malevolent, and the light gleamed on a high, belligerent forehead. The block captain, Guy decided, prowling with a highly personal hunger for convict tartare. Guy turned to run but met only pitiless iron bars.

Guy began to shake uncontrollably as the figure drew nearer, step by fiendish step, the foully disfigured face in shadow. The sweat pooled in the small of Guy's back as he made out a crude paddle of some sort dangling from the mad ogre's grip.

Uh-oh, thought Guy, wide awake for the very first time in his life. I'm going to die, he realized, this is horrible! Guy decided to begin praying immediately. I'll be so good! he promised God. I'll wake up early! I'll be nicer to my parents! I'll get a real job! I'll wear clean clothes! I'll never dye my hair! I'll make Venice wear clothes! I'll make Licky vacuum! I'll make Danilo chase things, like a dog should! I'll take care of all the poor people and sick people in the whole world! I'll end war! No more dancing! No more shopping! No more sleeping!

This last promise snapped Guy to his senses. It's useless, Guy knew. I've got to sleep! I'm a worthless human being! It's my calling! I'm ready to die!

A second more and the mastodon of doom would be upon him. Guy touched his hair and hoped against hope that he had not developed any pimples, so often the product of stress. Guy was determined to look good, to show some flair, even as he faced the Reaper, the dark usher's directions to the nearest exit. Guy wished he had a cigarette, or his sunglasses, some emblem of nonchalance. I'm so bad at this, Guy thought! The ogre approached.

"Hi . . . " Guy whispered, haltingly.

"Son," said Mr. Huber, waving his tennis racket. "Good to see you."

"Dad?" said Guy, incredulous. "Gee, is that you?"

23

Minimum Security

"You look well, son," said Guy's father. "Did you just get in? Good trip?"

Guy's father stood in the cellblock, facing his son in the dingy corridor. Mr. Huber was wearing a uniform identical to Guy's. The older man seemed in fine spirits, even a bit peppier than usual. He was testing his backhand with practice swats. Guy had no idea his father had been sent to prison. Was the entire family in disgrace?

"Dad," Guy asked. "Um, I don't want to . . . I mean, it's your business and everything, but . . . gee, Dad, *what are you doing here?*"

"Some sort of tax evasion nonsense," said Mr. Huber. "Hasn't your mother mentioned anything? Well, she's been busy, with the Larger and whatnot. I didn't want to bother you with it; I know you've got exams coming up. Been hittin' the books?"

Guy decided not to question any of his father's remarks. The

Hubers always respected one another's privacy. Prying only led to scenes and invariably spoiled the evening meal. Seconds earlier, Guy had expected to be molested, throttled, dismembered by a Big House beast; his father's presence was a wholly unexpected comfort.

"Got yourself a haircut, I see," Mr. Huber told his son approvingly. "Just the ticket. You were getting a tad shaggy around the collar; best not to let it get away from you. Now you're a regular gent!"

Guy leaned against a concrete wall and collected his thoughts.

"But Dad," Guy said, trying not to sound negative, "I mean, we're in prison. Isn't it really horrible? Boy, which one of these cells is yours?" Guy pointed to the rows of desolate enclosures.

"What?" said Mr. Huber. "Son, don't be ridiculous. No one lives out here, these are for storage."

Peering behind the bars, Guy saw this was true. The cells were filled with cardboard boxes and piles of yellowing party decorations.

"Your mother wrote me, she mentioned you'd be coming aboard," said Mr. Huber. "We'll be sharing a suite. Bunkin' in!"

Mr. Huber led Guy through the rear door of the cellblock. Beyond the door lay a long, fluorescent-lit room painted an institutional mint green. The room was crowded with ping-pong tables, battered leather couches and wood-grain formica coffee tables, strewn with news magazines in plastic sleeves. Mr. Huber hiked rapidly through this room, which was deserted except for Guy and his father.

"This is the old lounge," said Mr. Huber. "A bit shabby. The new space is just about finished, so they tell me. Quite spiffy, from all I hear. I hope we're not in for too much of that Italian business—those awful chairs."

Guy and his father left the lounge, passing into a gymnasium. This facility was spanking new and the very model of a contemporary health palace. The floor was carpeted in a sweeping purple broadloom, and the walls were blazingly mirrored. Redwood tubs bursting with foliage anchored soothing batik wall hangings. The mood was spa-like.

"Fine setup," Mr. Huber commented. "All very up-to-date. We'll get you on the machines, work on those abs."

"Those abs?" said Guy, lost.

"Abdominals," said Mr. Huber, patting his rippling stomach. Mr. Huber gestured to a shimmering grove of chrome machines, resembling outsize food processors, primed to mince and chop. These machines featured contoured cowhide seats, which the enthusiast straddled. A web of cams and pulleys then came into play, rotating and flexing the victim's limbs into taut perfection.

Guy found the gymnasium terrifying. He could imagine himself churning away, trapped within a steely mechanism; his heavily muscled corpse would be discovered still pumping, days later.

"They've got fellows here, instructors," Mr. Huber told his flinching son. "They'll keep you hoppin'. Top-notch team. I've never felt better, I'm like a boy again. How's your game?" Mr. Huber asked, feinting at Guy with his tennis racket.

"Gee, you mean tennis?" asked Guy. "I don't really like tennis all that much . . ."

"Not to worry," said Mr. Huber. "We'll get you in the league, keep you off your duff. None of your lollygagging now. Remember, son, you're in prison."

Mr. Huber led Guy out of the gymnasium and into a cobblestone courtyard. A brace of tidy thatched cottages sat at pleasing angles off the courtyard, forming a picturesque Tyrolean village. The whimsical huts were trimmed with geranium-filled window-boxes, scrollwork shutters and brass doorknockers. Guy half expected shepherds in period dress to appear, guiding docile flocks. Each cottage had a name, carved into a slice of raw birch nailed over the front door. The cottage titles included "Doin' Time," "Bide-A-Wee" and "Jailbird's Roost." Mr. Huber took Guy into one called "Bad Boys."

Guy was certain that dwarfs would be in residence, but the interior of the cottage proved to be thoroughly modern, spotless and well-appointed. Guy was shown to his room, a cheerful studio with bed, desk, bath and kitchenette. The cottage included Mr. Huber's quarters and a third studio as yet unoccupied. The furniture was molded plastic in primary colors, or blond wood. An abundance of swiveling architect's lamps and butcher block lent the suite an air of budget student housing.

Guy checked the TV in his room and spun the lighting dimmers. After washing up, he wandered out to join his father, who'd promised to take Guy for a light snack.

"Off we go," said Mr. Huber, now wearing a comfortable quilted smoking jacket over his uniform and carrying a pipe, very much the local squire. "There are some people I'd like you to meet. Let's put our best foot forward; I'm sure you'll find your niche. I believe everyone's at the pool."

The Huber men left their cottage and strolled down a flagstone path set in a manicured greensward. The path led toward the tower that Guy had glimpsed upon his arrival, a tower from which diving platforms now clearly jutted. The path was lined with carriage lamps set on poles and fitted with bulbs with flickering filaments, in imitation of candlelight.

The Olympic-scale pool was installed behind a gracefully modeled hillock. The pool was landscaped as a pond, its borders and filtration system disguised in natural rock formations. The water was heated, and lit from below. In the cool evening air, swirls of mist rose from the glassy surface. The chain-link fences that surrounded the outer prison had been erected to discourage the curious. Here they were modified to a weathered rail structure, for a New England charm. The guards, lolling in slatted, whitewashed towers, toted golf bags, which Guy had mistaken earlier for riflery.

No one was swimming, due to the chill, but a few convicts took dips after their saunas, plunging with shouts and splashes into the still water. Groups of men clustered at bar carts and gaily striped canvas cabanas. The men were enjoying flaming shish kebab and tropical punch served in coconut shells, as the prison chef was currently indulging in an "International Smorgasbord." The prisoners wore a variety of garments—clamdiggers, caftans and terry-lined shaving coats, mostly of the same dun-colored fabric as Guy's uniform.

"Dad, I'm not dressed," said Guy, turning to leave.

"Trust your old man," said Mr. Huber, dropping a barbecue apron over Guy's head. The apron was emblazoned with the phrase "Kiss the Cook," the motto printed alongside jitterbugging hamburger patties and fluffy buns with big red puckered lips.

"Buzz," said Mr. Huber, greeting a man in tweed cap, argyle vest and windowpane knickers.

"Dick," replied the man, the former head of an airline, convicted of immense fraud and four hundred counts of perjury, "we missed you at the lecture this afternoon."

"I'm sorry," said Mr. Huber. "I don't trust those young Turks, or Merrill Lynch. I'm considering a money market, but I'm no daredevil. Once burned."

"Suit yourself, skipper," said the man. "Who's this? New doubles partner?"

"Buzz," said Mr. Huber, with great pride, "this is my boy, my youngest. Guy, I'd like you to meet Tarwoodly Keith. He plays with Duff Pickling."

"Gee, the attorney general?" said Guy.

"Call me Buzz," said Tarwoodly Keith. "Dick, he's a fine boy."

As Guy surveyed the prison's population, at the pool and over the next few days, a pattern emerged. Guy decided to consult his father during their massage.

"Dad," Guy asked, as they writhed beneath the masseuse's crippling embrace, "I've been wondering something. Where are the crooks? Everybody seems to be here for, like, embezzlement, or graft, or copyright infringement or something. Didn't anybody, I don't know, kill anybody?"

"Well, let me see," Mr. Huber gasped, "ummmmpphh! Lower, Lotte, yes, that's it . . . Well, there are a few fellows in for third-degree manslaughter."

"That sounds great!" said Guy. "What is it?"

"Well, for example," Mr. Huber replied, "when a fellow kills his wife and the murder weapon is an antique. And we have Dutworth, Princeton type, his wife passed on in a hunting accident, although she was found in a negligee. It's all very complex, fine legal points. But everyone's being rehabilitated, really getting on with it. So we don't like to call our people murderers."

"Oh, I see," said Guy. "Okay. Gee, what should we call them?"

"Widowers," said Mr. Huber. "Oooooh, Lotte—son, isn't Lotte a gem? Lotte, if I weren't married to the most wonderful gal on God's green earth, I swear . . ."

"Dad," said Guy, still puzzled. "Does anybody here ever, I don't know, riot or anything?"

"Well, there was some difficulty, a bit of a contretemps," Mr. Huber recalled, "a week ago, something about the shrimp. Seems it wasn't fresh."

"But I don't get it," said Guy, still struggling. "Why is everybody here so nice? I mean, rich?"

"Son," said Mr. Huber patiently. "This is Minimum Security. We can't simply plop poor fellows into the mix, people without our advantages. They wouldn't know how to behave. They would be uncomfortable. They wouldn't know anyone. They're fine fellows, I'm sure, every last manjack, but we mustn't force these things. Argggghhh, that's it, right there . . . Lotte, you're a *genius.*"

As Guy mingled, he found his fellow prisoners amiable and only slightly tedious. The experience was not unlike attendance at one of his parents' parties, and the guest lists did overlap considerably. In addition to athletics, Guy was forced to participate in many naggingly rigorous modes of rehabilitation, including writing to his mother and theater-going (the Pokey Players in mop wigs and balloon breasts, whooping up *School for Scandal* and *Star-Spangled Girl*). Seminars were also available, and Guy sandwiched in Country Découpage and the Nosh Yourself Thin series.

Gradually, Guy settled in. He tried to remain chipper, although he was afflicted with the loneliness common to any novice at summer camp. I miss Venice, Guy thought. And I miss Licky, and the Club, and everything. I don't like prison, Guy decided, it's too Connecticut.

24

Cellmates

After a month in prison, Guy's tennis game improved. At his father's urging, Guy spent long hours with the prison pro, perfecting his serve and trying not to throw his racket onto the clay every few minutes out of nausea and frustration.

On a balmy April morning, Guy found himself enrolled in an entry-level singles tournament. His first few matches went well, as he was pitted against a squadron of elderly men, their incarceration the result of an anti-trust action earlier in the decade.

As the day wore on, Guy grew half-demented with fatigue. His later opponents proved more agile, and Guy was forced to cover the full court, darting relentlessly, wearing himself to a frazzle. Guy still hated tennis. He felt that one of the players in any sport should be allowed to use a gun.

As Guy was about to drop, to reincarnate as a puddle of warm perspiration, he experienced a vision. Glancing off the court toward a concrete plaza, his mind invented the most extraordinary mirage. He imagined a café surrounded by a low hedge and sprinkled with round white metal tables, each with a pinwheel umbrella stuck at the center. Blasé spectators sat at some of these tables, in twos and threes, wearing visors and sipping slushy margaritas through straws. A central table, however, was positively deluged with prisoners, gathering three deep, completely obliterating the table from view. The men were laughing and chattering, and, from somewhere deep within their ranks, Guy could swear he detected a familiar voice.

"Darlings," the voice inquired, "isn't anyone going to get me something nice and cool?"

Guy was certain he was mistaken, perhaps sunstruck. This could not be his beloved. Cigarette smoke curled over the hidden table, and Guy decided to risk a closer investigation. He limped to the table, squirming his way through the pack of babbling prisoners.

"It's about time," Venice remarked, as Guy appeared.

"Venice!" said Guy, overjoyed, his strength returning instantly.

Venice stood up. She was wearing a man's white T-shirt and a baseball cap, an outfit she considered suitable for a country visit. She put her arms around Guy's neck and kissed him. Eight men stood patiently, holding Venice's cocktails.

"This is so great!" said Guy. "But what are you doing here?" Was this still prison, Guy wondered, or were co-ops now available? Had Venice committed a suitably polite crime? Had the new Michelin Guide been published, awarding the prison commissary an additional star?

"They called me," said Venice. "Thanks, Stu."

Venice accepted a frozen margarita with a tiny paper umbrella in it.

"Wait, who called you?" asked Guy.

"The prison," Venice continued, tasting her drink. "Aren't these lethal? I'm part of a program. Conjugal visits. Could you die?"

"Conjugal visits?" said Guy, wonderingly.

"Darling, it's madness," Venice explained. "They want wives and girlfriends to come to the prison and keep you boys happy. It's all supposed to be terribly natural and humane, so you won't all turn into savage creatures or start dating each other. So I said, 'By all means, let me pack a bag.' I told the warden, 'Darling, I am going to rehabilitate my husband until his brains fall out.' "

"RAYYY!!!" cheered the nearby prisoners, saluting Venice's dedication. "RAYYYY!!! RAYYYY!!!"

"Men behind bars," said Venice. "Too much."

"Venice, this is wonderful!" said Guy. "Come on, I'll show you my room! And all my stuff!"

Guy and Venice disentangled themselves from the crowd at the tennis courts and walked toward Guy's cottage, hand in hand under the leafy maples. A procession of inmates followed, toting Venice's twenty-six pieces of luggage on their heads, as native bearers. The grounds crew, mowing and pruning, kept a discreet distance as the Hubers discussed Guy's life in the hoosegow.

"Has it been just unbearable," Venice asked, "or is it fun?"

"It's pretty bad," said Guy. "Next week I have to go horseback riding."

"Oh, no," said Venice, shocked. "Can they do that to you? Isn't it, you know, cruel and unusual?"

"Gee, I don't know," said Guy. "Did you get the ashtray I sent you? You know, the mosaic one?"

"Yes," Venice giggled. "Everyone died. Did you get my postcard?"

"It was great," said Guy, "but the warden got it first and crossed everything out. I guess they censor stuff."

"*I* did that," said Venice, "so you'd think it was really filthy. Well, hello, Walt."

Venice was discovering so many familiar faces at the prison. When the conjugal questionnaires had been distributed, a surprising number of convicts had requested Venice's visit, identifying her as a spouse or mistress. The remaining prisoners had claimed Ratallia Parv in a similar fashion, with a smattering of bids for Jon Gelle.

"Now, Guy," Venice asked, in her huskiest tones, "just how much rehabilitation will you need? Have you become desperately anti-social? Are you all but lost to decent society?"

"I think so," said Guy, brutally. "I think I'm almost beyond hope. You're my last chance of leading a normal life, and paying my debt to the good people of New York State and America."

"Well," Venice concluded, "we'd better get started. Cruel and unusual," she repeated, musingly. "Words to live by."

As Guy and Venice neared the cottage colony, they heard voices raised in the adjacent admissions rooms in the less progressive sector of the prison.

"Darling, what's going on?" Venice asked Guy. "Are they electrocuting someone?"

"Gee, I don't think so," said Guy, considering the question, and the larger issue of capital punishment itself. "It would ruin the TV reception."

The brawl intensified, and someone could be heard screaming and flinging metal objects about, the violence resounding throughout the tri-state area.

"It sounds wild," said Venice. "We've got to go see. Just a peek."

"But I want to get all rehabilitated," Guy moaned beseechingly. Guy, after all, had not been rehabilitated for many months now, discounting his daily attempts at self-help.

"Soon," Venice promised, sympathetically. "Calm down."

. . .

Guy and Venice entered the admissions area, tracing the outcry to the prison barber's cubicle, where Guy's streak had fallen in his bleak, early hours at the facility. Guy and Venice peeked into the cubicle and witnessed a sorry spectacle indeed. A new inmate, raw with rebellion, was pummeling the prison barber and pitching scissors and clippers into the hall.

"DARLING!" the inmate howled at the prison barber, "I said I want a MOHAWK, this is NOT a MOHAWK, this is a CREWCUT, where else have you WORKED?"

"Darling," said Venice. "Howdy."

"Hi, Licky!" said Guy, somehow not surprised to find the peevish servant in custody. "What's wrong?"

"GUY!" cried Licky. "VENICE! Thank the blessed LORD. LOOK at me, isn't it tear-dripping and PATHETIC? He could fix it in a SECOND but he WON'T, he's pure GEEK, I told him, you shave the sides and leave a brush in the center, it's BASIC. And he won't color, I mean, where ARE we?"

"Darling, may I?" asked Venice, scooping the clippers up off the floor.

"Please," whimpered the stricken barber. "Anything."

Licky righted the stool he'd overturned, curtsied and sat. Venice then deftly shaved the remaining hair from both sides of Licky's head, leaving a shrieking ridge along the center. Inspired, she also removed one of Licky's eyebrows. This inaugurated a fad that left the entire prison with a look of heightened skepticism, as if one brow had been raised into the stratosphere.

"Hair," said Venice, inspecting her handiwork. "It's my life."

"*Merci,*" said Licky, looking in the mirror. "*You* have a future. *Comprende?*" he said to the barber, who sat huddled in a corner, clutching a tin of talcum. "There is hair," Licky opined, "and then there is *coiffure.* NOW I can go anywhere. I'll be back in a week, for my stubble."

. . .

Guy took Venice and Licky back to the Huber cottage, where Licky was installed in the vacant studio. The three settled in for a light lunch of cheese and fruit.

Venice nibbled a peach. "Darling, I don't mean to get all nosy," she asked Licky, "but what are you in for?"

"Oh my dears," sighed Licky, "it's too ridiculous. You won't believe it. I'm mortified. I mean, cancel my pedicure, seat me by the kitchen, let's all eat some worms. Worms *flambé*. I was arrested for, now catch this, I, your simple domestic mouth-piece, was arrested for selling drugs to children."

"Really?" said Guy, wolfing a Triscuit. "That's terrible. Boy. Did you do it?"

"Guy," said Licky, profoundly wounded. "GUY HUBER. I did not sell drugs to helpless, innocent children, creatures still possessing several unaided senses, their neurons as yet unmolested by pill or potion. *Nay.* "

"Darling, of course not," soothed Venice.

"I *gave* them to them," said Licky.

"That's what I thought," said Guy. "I mean, I knew you wouldn't take advantage."

"And the sad thing," said Licky, "the truly wrenching detail, is that the cops, afterwards, they wouldn't even let the kids keep it. I mean, I was walking down Madison, at around one, and there were all these adorable little kids on a field trip from kindergarten—you know, in pairs, with name tags and bag lunches and little mittens attached to their sleeves. It was heaven, I think they were taking them to Cartier.

"Anyway, so they stop at a red light, and these two little boys start arguing, because one has a teeny bit of hash left, and he wouldn't share. And I can't help listening, and I say, 'Little boy, just what kind of behavior is that?' So I give his little friend a toot, just to, you know, even things out. And they were so happy, the teacher thanked me, the homeroom mothers thanked me, and then this cop comes over and just goes mondo. I said, 'Officer, please, get off my dress.'

"So the kids start crying, and the homeroom moms start thwacking the cop, but then the light changes and everybody leaves, and here I am. Life in these here United States. I ask you."

"Darling, it's an outrage," said Venice. "It's too criminal."

"More Brie?" asked Guy, gently.

Licky went to bed fairly early that night, tuckered from the journey to the prison and his first session in the gymnasium. Guy and Venice were nestled cosily in Guy's bed, as they had been for many hours. The sex had been phenomenal. Venice had realized a universal fantasy, love with a convict. Not bad, she thought, cradled in Guy's arms. She noticed that Guy had begun to mark off the days of his confinement in bright crayon on the wall beside the bed; Guy had gotten carried away and added some clouds and an apple tree.

"Do you feel rehabilitated yet?" Venice asked, biting Guy's neck.

"I don't know," said Guy, nuzzling Venice's shoulder. "I'm a hardened criminal."

"Are you kids all right?" asked Mr. Huber, tapping on Guy's door. "Do you need anything from the deli?"

"We're fine, Dad," Guy called out.

"Goodnight, Dick," called Venice.

"Venice . . ." Guy murmured, as his father's footsteps died out.

"Mmmmm . . ." Venice replied.

"I think I need more rehabilitation," Guy decided. "I think I need lots more."

"Definitely," Venice agreed. "You're backsliding."

"Stop me," Guy begged, kissing Venice's hip, "before I kill again."

25

Torture

Soon Guy, Venice and Licky grew bored with their term at prison, the standard result of any resort situation. There were so many activities scheduled hourly at the facility, and yet there was nothing to do. The group was soon reduced to non-stop tanning at poolside. They would oil at noon, in order to lasso the peak tanning hours, and splay themselves on chaises at the water's edge. They would review each other's color at regular intervals, turning their bodies for an even coat, *cordon bleu* chefs timing the roast. As the afternoon wore on, they rolled their chaises, trailing the sun. Other convicts would set their watches, guided by the position of Guy and his friends at the pool.

Somewhere in early June, Guy found himself at mid-umber, serenaded by blue jays and the water's easeful rippling. A cordial breeze whispered its way across his skin.

"It's weird, I don't think I like nature," Guy said. He scratched his nose, flaking off a bit of zinc oxide.

"What, darling?" asked Venice, without moving. Venice lay beside Guy, her face shaded by a large straw hat, defending her complexion from the sun's vengeance. Otherwise she was wrapped in approximately two ounces of spandex.

"I said, I think I hate nature," Guy reiterated. He kept his eyes shut as he continued. "I'm a terrible person. You know, yesterday, when I went on that nature hike? Up into the mountains? Well, it was all, like, really pretty and everything. And all the plants had labels on them, and these deer and squirrels kept popping out, they were so sweet. And then we got to the top of the mountain, and everybody was going, 'Ooh, look at that,' and, 'Oh, what a great view.'

"So I looked out, and you could see everything, all the trees and the sky, right down to the ocean. And I stared at it, right, like you're supposed to, and I thought, Wow, this is really, like, exalted and magnificent and everything. And I thought, If I have to look at it for one more second, I'm going to scream."

"Nature isn't dull, darling," said Venice. "Don't be silly. Nature is mean. I was out on the golf course this morning, with Archie Tablemere and Kenny Hibble and Les and Hunt and those boys, and it was the worst. I just sat in the golf cart, and I still got all these mosquito bites and grass stains and freckles. I kept saying to myself, 'Darling, you're not a freckled sort of person,' but they just kept happening. And I can't wear anything decent to cover up the freckles, not out here. Just shorts and backpacks and things. Guy, yesterday your father told me I looked healthy. *Healthy.* I said, Dick, you watch that. Is my back done?"

"You're such infants," sniffed Licky. Licky was stretched out on the diving board, bronzed and glistening, with lemon juice soaking his hair for natural highlighting.

"Don't blame nature, my dears," he continued, "just because your lives are wretched. Blame this place. I mean, I've dreamed of going to prison, ever since I was a baby. It sounded fabulous, an absolute utopia. But, I ask you, where are the men?"

"The men?" said Guy, puzzled. "But Licky, there are lots of guys here."

"No, dear," Licky replied, "I'm not talking about guys. I'm talking about men. Thrill slayers. Repeat offenders. Caged meat. You know—tattoos, and brain damage. Dreamboats. I mean, I watch those TV shows—where is the sexual slavery? Where is the wholesale barter of human souls? Where is the murderer who will trade my body for a pack of Newports?"

"Darling, what about the guards?" asked Venice. "Haven't you met anyone?"

"The guards?" Licky ranted. "The *guards?* Now, you know how I feel about uniforms. I mean, I *tingle.* Jackboots. Sam Brown belts. Nightsticks. Give me a man with mirrored sunglasses and a sneer, and I'm happy. But what do I get around here? Have you seen these people? They're all grad students in penal reform. With briefcases. And ponytails. They keep asking me if I want to join an encounter group or a rap session. I tried one, and everyone was sitting around using hand puppets, acting out their problems with authority figures. It's like a day-care center."

"It's like a weekend at the beach," Venice decided, "Where you think it's going to be fun, and then you're trapped. Suddenly everyone's playing Scrabble and collecting seashells."

"Gee, what do you think is going on in the city right now?" Guy asked, dreamily.

"The city," Venice sighed. "Stop it."

"Don't tease," said Licky.

"Where's Danilo?" Guy asked. "Is he still in town?"

"Yes," said Venice. "I put him in a hotel."

"A *hotel,*" Licky swooned. *"Imagine."*

"Room service," Venice ached.

"Lobbies," said Guy.

"Asphalt," said Licky.

"TAXIS!" everyone moaned in unison.

"Come on, guys," said Guy, trying to cool things down. "It's not so bad out here. I mean, not really."

"That's true," said Venice, trying to be helpful, "there's archery."

"And singing great old campfire songs," Guy added.

"You're right," Licky agreed. "I mean, if we have to stay out here for a while longer, it won't be the end of the world. I mean, there are worse things."

"There's tornadoes," Guy suggested.

"And cellulite," said Venice.

"And having your fingernails pulled out with a pair of pliers," said Guy.

"BUT AT LEAST THOSE THINGS AREN'T BORING!" Licky screamed.

Licky had finally said it; he had employed the most damning epithet in his vocabulary. Licky feared boredom. He would try anything to avoid the mundane, the harrowingly tedious, the convulsively humdrum.

"We've got to do something," Licky announced, "or we're going to start peeling."

"Tonight is Square Dancing," Venice shuddered. "Again."

"But what can we do?" asked Guy, desperately.

"Scoot," said Licky.

"What?" asked Guy.

"Hightail it," said Licky. "Go over the wall. Check-out time."

"Really?" considered Guy, taken with the idea. "You really think we could?"

"A prison break," said Venice, pleased as could be. "Well, why *not?*"

2 6

A Daring Escape

After the peak tanning hours drew to a close, Guy, Venice and Licky returned to their cottage. They were determined to escape, whatever the cost in human life.

"What will we need?" asked Guy urgently.

"Stockings," said Licky, hatching an infallible stratagem. "We'll need disguises."

Venice opened a drawer and yanked out all her hosiery. A disguise is more of a necessity in bank robbery, but Licky had trouble differentiating between crimes.

"I *cannot* wear taupe," said Licky, discarding stocking after stocking. "My *reputation.*"

"This is so exciting!" said Guy, sorting the pantyhose. "We're going over the wall!"

"Oh, Guy," said Venice. "You're such a pushover."

The group finally settled on classic black sheers.

Mr. Huber returned to the cottage after a good nine holes and found the suite's inhabitants swathed in nylon.

"What's all this?" said Mr. Huber. "Frat initiation? Lord, what a time we used to have. Every year, right before Homecoming, we'd pile into a Packard and charge up to Cambridge. We'd filch the Harvard marching band's big bass drum! We'd ransom it! Hooligans!"

"We're breaking out, Dad," said Guy. "It's going to be great! Do you want to come?"

"Son, I'd love to," said Mr. Huber, "but tonight's Square Dancing. I'd hate to miss it."

Once a week, the prison sponsored a hootenanny. The commissary was strewn with bales of hay, Japanese lanterns were strung about, and punch was served from a tin washtub. Local women trundled in homemade pies and eligible daughters. The warden called the dances. This week, he planned to instruct the inmates in the intricate footwork of the Cotton-Eyed Joe.

"Oh, Dad," said Guy, rolling his eyes in the habit of embarrassed children the world over.

"You're sweet," said Venice, giving Mr. Huber a peck on the cheek, through the mesh of her stocking.

"Dick," said Licky, "someday I'm gonna marry you."

Guy, Venice and Licky packed their belongings and arranged to have them freighted back to the loft. After dinner they could detect the fiddler tuning up for the barn dance, and they agreed that it was time to make their move. They donned their stockings; their heads resembling three black nylon turnips, they began their perilous trek to freedom, their liberation mile.

"Is this dangerous?" asked Guy, enraptured. "Are we going to be shot in our tracks?"

The group left the cottage and passed through the admissions area, on tiptoe.

"Hello, darling," said Venice, nodding her shrouded head at a guard.

"You never call me," the guard whined.

"It's been fabby-do," Licky said, brushing past the prison psychologist. "Should we tip?" Licky whispered to Guy.

"We'll send something," Guy whispered back. "A bottle of wine."

The trio pressed on. They waved to the prison barber, who now displayed a photograph of Licky's hairstyle in his cubicle. "I've given him a whole new life," said Licky.

The supply room, the laundry, the prison yard—all fell past.

"Where is everyone?" Venice asked, slightly miffed. "I get more attention when I leave a phone booth."

They crept ahead, leaving the prison and approaching the main gate.

"My nose itches," said Guy. "It's all smushed."

"Halt!" shouted the guard at the gate, hoisting his M-1 and pointing it at the group, the safety latch disengaged.

"Oh, stop it," said Venice, as she breezed by.

"Headache," said Guy, jerking his thumb at Venice, and sharing a "Women! Go figure!" grimace with the guard.

"After Labor Day," Licky told the guard, "we'll *sit* on the phone. I want to hear *everything.*"

"We had a really nice time," said Guy to the guard, dutifully.

Venice paused for a second and looked at the guard. Despite the stocking over her head, the guard dropped his rifle and had to be forcibly prevented from falling on his bayonet.

"Bye, darling!" said Venice, satisfied at last.

They reached the main road and tore the stockings from their heads. They were miles from the nearest town. The prison was surrounded by farms and lonely highway; all anyone could see were countless telephone poles and stars. There were no cars on the road, and the only sounds were of crickets and distant Hawaiian guitar. If the escaping convicts were not smack in the middle of nowhere, they were certainly nearby.

"We made it!" Venice shouted, grabbing Guy for a victory squeeze.

"We're on the lam!" said Guy, jumping up and down.

"Taxi!" yelled Licky, always the clearer head.

There was a screech, and a spray of gravel hit Guy in the ankle. A Checker cab pulled up, with a dangling headlight and a yawning driver.

"Darling," said Venice to the cabbie as she opened the car door, "are you free?"

"All yours, babydoll," said the cabbie as Guy climbed in the back seat with Venice. Licky hopped in front beside the driver, a man of pungent appeal.

"Well, *hello,*" said Licky, scrutinizing the driver's hack license, posted on the dashboard with his photo. "You take a *heaven* picture. Are these *your* children?" he asked, examining a Polaroid propped against a magnetized hula figurine.

"Where ya headed?" asked the cabbie, scratching his forehead.

"The Club de, please!" said Guy, unable to keep the leaping elation from his tone. "Downtown!"

27

Return to the Fabulous Club de

Guy and Venice slept most of the way back into Manhattan in order to arrive fully recharged at the Club de. Licky spent the journey chatting with the cabbie, absorbing substantial data on toilet training, the cost of children's shoes, and the homosexual menace. The cab approached the city limits at close to midnight. The timing was ideal.

As the cab barreled onto the Club de's block, Licky noticed something decidedly askew. There were no cars in front of the Club, no limousine pileup, no sardinelike gridlock of taxis and Cadillacs and tourist charters.

"Wake up," Licky told Guy and Venice. "We're here, I think."

Guy peered out the window of the taxi as Venice changed into a fresh outfit in the back seat. Venice could change anywhere, slithering out of one look and dragging another over her head, all elbows and engineering. This process always caused cabdrivers to take a sudden and severe interest in adjusting their rear-view mirrors.

For a moment, Guy became convinced that the Club was closed for the evening, shuttered due to holiday or natural disaster. There was no crowd hungering at the door, no bloated, ravenous monster raising its thousand dripping heads and screeching for entrance. The aluminum stanchions were more or less in place, but the velvet rope hung slack and unneeded. Four people stood outside the rope. Guy was not sure if these four people were waiting for admittance or had just emerged or were loitering. There was no desperation about them, no wild hope, no propulsion in any direction. They could have been anywhere.

Guy, Venice and Licky left the cab and approached the rope. Renzo stepped out of the Club and Guy was reassured by the familiar face and immutable bulk.

"Hi, Renzo!" Guy called. "How are you?"

"Awright," Renzo replied. "Howya doin'?"

"We're great!" said Guy.

"I'm back," said Venice, giving Renzo a quick kiss.

"Gee, what's going on?" asked Guy.

"Not much," said Renzo, with as much wistfulness as a man who has swallowed human noses can muster.

"Darling, who's on the door?" Licky asked.

"Some guy," Renzo replied after thinking for a moment. "I think he's inside, or maybe he went out for a smoke or somethin'. He's around. Ya comin' in?"

"Sure," said Guy. "Did you miss us?"

"Yeah," said Renzo, fully forlorn, digging his toe into the sidewalk, "it's been kinda off around here. For a coupla weeks now."

"Darling, did something happen?" asked Venice.

"Nah," said Renzo, sniffling, and wiping his nose on the building, "nothin' really."

. . .

The group entered the Club. Everything seemed as it had been, the mirrors, the palms, the atmosphere of a gilded, shadowy boudoir. But the coatcheck was now staffed by a single efficient young lady. She smiled pertly and took everyone's wrap, passing the plastic checks promptly over the counter. The previous coatcheck employees had been peerlessly vacant, artlessly rude, superior in the tradition of girls for whom chipped fingernails constitutes holocaust. This new young lady wore a neatly ironed blouse and a serious barrette that tidied her helmet of shiny, mouse-brown hair. This was the sort of young lady hired from an agency, a Gal Friday schooled in Making a Good First Impression and Maintaining Office Morale.

"Have a pleasant evening," the young lady chirped, with the automaton twinkle of an airline stewardess.

"Darling," advised Licky, staring fixedly at this young lady, "I think it's time for that enema."

Guy led the way into the body of the Club. The bartenders had been replaced as well. The ridiculously strapping, agreeably dense jocks had been banished. In their place were more agency types, weary middle-aged men in short-sleeved, white nylon shirts with black clip-on bow ties.

"What'll it be, mac?" one of the bartenders asked Guy.

Guy did not answer. He was distracted, examining the crowd. The Club was full, and the music had attained its customary blare and thump. Guy looked at the dancers and the drinkers, at the men and women lolling on the banquettes. He blinked and looked again. He did not know a soul.

"Darling, who are these people?" Venice asked, equally puzzled.

Where was Contessa Larini? Tanzo Matta? Caronia? Where were the nightcrawlers, the old faces, the lifted faces, the genderless *monde,* the dazed, dashing glitterati?

Where were the people who know just how to cover their

faces when the photographers arrive and yet still be recogniz-able in the picture? Where were the people willing to spend their last three thousand dollars on two yards of fabric? The people who care deeply about the correct way to lean against an archway? The people who talk about sex in terms of trends? Where were the people who, given a choice between a poor hair-cut and the loss of a loved one, would need a minute?

Where were the people who created themselves painstakingly from magazine photos and sheet music and irony? Where was everybody?

"Oh my God," said Licky, focusing, *"look."*

They looked. The crowd at the Club, at first glance, appeared as expected—the fashions, the movements, the illegal sub-stances. On closer inspection, everyone was a bit off, a frame out of synch, a faded or too loud facsimile. The clothing was ill-fitting or manufactured in shiny chemical equivalents of the original fibers. The new faces were happy but blurred, charac-terless puddings, dopey donuts, anyone's faces.

With a start, Guy began to recognize these faces. These were the people who used to wait outside. The funseekers. The mob at the door. Guy stared at these people. They looked perfectly normal, he realized. They were just people, nice people; they carried no dread virus. They were not inferior, a lesser race. They were just amateurs.

These people lacked the commitment of Guy's set. These peo-ple rose at 7 a.m. for a nourishing breakfast. These people went out at most two evenings per month. These people had bad backs and day jobs and families and better things to do. They did not live for the night, nor did they wish to. They visited the Club de to satisfy their curiosity. They danced to a song or two, they downed a Lite beer and they turned in early.

Even Debbie could detect a fluctuation in the Club's ambience. She, Bruce and Michelle had returned to the city for the first

time since their fateful masquerade. Tonight they had been ushered into the Club without hesitation. They had been welcomed,
they had been received as honored guests, as desirables. Debbie
was immediately suspicious. While she was pleased at gaining
entrance, some essential surge was lacking, some sense of
gooseflesh, of trophy, of immeasurable social triumph, of style
rewarded. Why are they letting *me* in, Debbie wondered.

Once inside the Club, the Jerseyans became increasingly
bewildered. Debbie had remembered the Club's interior in a
burnished haze, as an intoxicating spin of hot lights, vampire
dusk and elegant freakishness, as a sultan's pavilion, as a velvet circus tent, stocked with undulant tigers wearing diamond
tiaras.

Now everything seemed so . . . possible. So acceptable. So
eager to please. For a moment, Debbie assumed that she had
not entered the actual Club de. She imagined that she had taken
a wrong turn and ended at a lesser nightspot, a reproduction,
a site still within the borders of her home state. Where were
all the people Debbie had read about in the tabloids, the people
who didn't quite have regular careers, or ages, or underwear?
Was the orgy in storage, or what? Is this *it?* Debbie speculated.
Is the Forbidden City really just a dingy small town?

"This place sucks," said Bruce, his hands on his hips.

"It's so teeny," commented Michelle, "and there's gum wrap-
pers on the floor."

"I LOVE IT," commanded Debbie. Debbie tried to sound au-
thoritative, but her words trailed off and were swamped by the
music, which now came across as monotonous and headachey
rather than compellingly crude. Debbie began to wish she'd
saved her new Tanzo Matta stone-washed, baggy-look, French-
cut jeans for a more special occasion.

Venice and Guy explored the Club and found only strangers.
The notorious lounges and parlors had grown oddly trite, over-

done, mutating into flimsy, painted backdrops for a varsity show. The upholstery had frayed, and the mirrors and tile were streaked with fingerprints. Everything was smaller than they remembered, and too fussy, too aggressively detailed. Even beloved artifice wears poorly.

Licky spent some time on the phone, but most of the people he called were out. Guy and Venice did not try to dance. Their limbs had become inexplicably awkward, leaden. The couple felt uncoordinated. They bumped into one another. Their rhythm was off.

The Club emptied on the early side, clearing out entirely by 2 a.m. People collected their last year's coats and left to retrieve sensible Japanese cars, with excellent gas mileage, handy for the long drive back to the boroughs. People discussed their jogging regimens and their insurance premiums as if they were exiting a PTA meeting, or the finals of a lackluster bowling tournament. The disc jockey packed up a little after 3 a.m. and went off to meet with his tax person.

The music ceased, and the Club was still. Hand in hand, Guy and Venice wandered out onto the dance floor, bedraggled babes lost in a thicket. Guy called out, checking for an echo, but the ricochet was swallowed in the blackness. The Club no longer held that crystalline, cutthroat blackness, the glamour of black mirror. Now the darkness was stagnant, smoggy, the useless gray of a looted tomb.

Guy felt dizzy. Thrown, he had to sit down. Venice joined him, kneeling at the center of the rutted, splintering dance floor. Guy tried to regain his balance by lying very still, with his head cradled in Venice's lap. Guy stared up at the lighting instruments high above. Most of these instruments were now dark. One or two glowed, as if they had been unplugged but would not fully extinguish for a few moments.

Licky also began to feel uncomfortable, off-kilter. He stood, requiring some physical activity to clear his head. He ran off, disappearing into the dark, aimed at the stairs.

"I'll be right back," Licky's disembodied voice called from somewhere. "I'm . . . I'm . . ."

Guy and Venice couldn't make out the rest of Licky's remark. In fact, Licky had not completed his thought. His chatter, his urge to amuse, had momentarily deserted him. For a second, Licky had nothing to say. The size of the room and its moribund emptiness frightened Licky. He lived for the intimate exchange, for the very best dirty secrets. Licky would remain silent rather than hurl repartee into the void.

"No more Club de," said Guy, feeling Venice's hand on his cheek.

"No more," said Venice. The couple seemed not unlike a pair of parting vacation soulmates on a final lingering day of August.

Guy rose. He walked across the dance floor and scaled the column that supported the disc jockey's booth. Guy stared at the dials and levers and turntables, at the buttons and needles and robot arms that produced the Club's incessant vibration. He flipped through a rack of albums.

Guy did not select a familiar song; such a choice seemed sloppy, easy, instant nostalgia for last Tuesday. Guy came across an album of Chopin. The record remained from a fashion show that had been staged at the Club some afternoon months before. Tanzo had selected classical accompaniment for his runway presentation, the music had functioned as a marvelous promotional gimmick.

Guy slipped the album onto the turntable. The delicate waltz began to fill the Club, sounding far better than Chopin could have intended, as the composer had lived in an era of rudimentary amplification.

"GROSS," shouted Venice from across the room. "What is this?"

"I don't know," said Guy, climbing down from the booth. "I found it. Tanzo used it."

"Of course," said Venice. "His boyfriend probably wrote it. He had to use it."

Guy held out his arms. Venice glided over, linking her hands behind his neck. Guy put his hands on Venice's waist. They began to move, merely rocking at first, keeping to a small corner of the dance floor.

Locating the beat, Guy and Venice began to waltz, somewhat jerkily. Neither had waltzed before, but they had seen movies, *Broadway Melodies* and *Nites in Old Vienna*. Guy liked the dance, the swooping dips, the balancing act. He liked holding Venice, keeping her from twirling off into the unknown. Venice threw her head back as the couple spun faster and faster, ransacking the floor, whooping at times, making themselves dizzy.

The music grew more somber, lamenting the close of a ball far less frenzied, far more polite than the life Guy and Venice preferred. The few remaining lights went out, erasing the contours of the room. The Club's sole illumination was now a thin band of purple neon circling the dance floor. Guy and Venice danced in blackness, guided only by one another. From afar, they resembled sparks or tiny, attractive planets sailing across a sleepy universe.

Venice leaned into Guy's body, and they clung to one another. Their waltz slowed, and Venice placed her head on Guy's chest. Finally they hardly moved, but stood, swaying, holding each other. Guy worried about the Club, about the structure itself, the walls and the floor and hallways. The poor Club de, Guy thought; it's an orphan. What if someone turns it into a warehouse, or a parking garage? Venice was imagining similar destinies for the Club—a conversion to office use, or a demolition.

"Yuk," said Venice tenderly, looking into Guy's eyes.

"Yuk-o-matic," said Guy, looking back, and they held each other some more.

A NOTE ON THE TYPE

This book was set in a digitized version of Bodoni Book, a type face named after Giambattista Bodoni (1740–1813), a celebrated printer and type designer of Rome and Parma. Bodoni Book as produced by the Linotype Company is not a copy of any one of Bodoni's fonts, but a composite, modern version of the Bodoni manner. Bodoni's innovations in type style included a greater degree of contrast in the thick and thin elements of the letters and a sharper and more angular finish of details.

Composed by the Haddon Craftsmen, Inc.
Scranton, Pennsylvania

Printed and bound by R. R. Donnelley
Harrisonburg, Virginia

Designed by Cecily Dunham